Blackjacks of Nevada

Five years in prison has given Cheyenne Brady plenty of time to dwell on revenge after being left for dead during a hold-up by the Nevada Blackjacks.

Upon his release Brady joins up with an old prospector, Sourdough Lamar, and together they head for Winnemucca, where Cheyenne has inherited a blacksmithing business from his father. But when Brady's old gang, led by Big-Nose Rafe Culpepper, plans to rob the town's bank, Cheyenne is accused of masterminding the hold-up. Can he extricate himself from once again sinking into a life of crime? Bullets fly in the showdown to resolve the issue.

Blackjacks of Nevada

Ethan Flagg

A Black Horse Western

ROBERT HALE · LONDON

ISBN 978-0-7198-1188-3

Robert Hale Limited
Clerkenwell House
Clerkenwell Green
London EC1R 0HT

www.halebooks.com

Typeset by
Derek Doyle & Associates, Shaw Heath
Printed and bound in Great Britain by
CPI Antony Rowe, Chippenham and Eastbourne

ONE

DOG FIGHT

The robbery of the overland stagecoach had gone according to plan. Information that it was carrying the monthly payroll to the miners of the Ruth copper mine in Nevada's White Pine Range was correct. The strong box was heavy, its contents filling three saddle-bags.

An upbeat Rafe Culpepper led his men back through the labyrinth of canyons to their hideout in the Monte Cristo Mountains.

Gabbs Hole was a secluded enclave surrounded on all sides by towering ramparts of orange sandstone. The only way in was by way of a narrow gorge. Interlaced pieces of brushwood latticework were positioned across the entrance to conceal it from the suspicious eyes of unwelcome interlopers. Not that any ventured into the network of twisting ravines that characterized the Monte Cristos: it was too easy to get lost.

Big-Nose Rafe had stumbled upon it by accident following the ambush of a pony-express rider back in the fall of 1860. At the time he was a young tearaway fleeing the scene of his first robbery and had become disorientated amidst the confusing terrain.

Once he had discovered the Hole, the astute outlaw fully appreciated that the place offered the perfect hideout. Backtracking, he devised a simple set of signs that would mean nothing to anyone else. They were scratched on to rocks, thus providing an easy means of locating the hideout quickly.

Gabbs Hole had since provided Culpepper with a safe bolthole that had always kept him one step ahead of the law. Now he led a criminal gang of his own, the members of which were known as the Blackjacks.

The gang leader had always harboured a yen to emulate the swashbuckling pirates of the Caribbean. A black skull and crossbones was worn across the front of his hat during every raid. This emblem made him feel like his hero, Robert Teech who was known to posterity as Blackbeard. The slick methods employed by the Blackjacks had made the gang notorious throughout the territory. Disappearing after each robbery, they had become a thorn in the side of the Nevada authorities.

Nobody had ever set eyes on any of the outlaws due to their leader's insistence that black masks be worn at all times during a heist. That way, none of their faces occupied a wanted dodger. Descriptions abounded alongside the growing rewards offered for their capture – dead or alive! But without positive identification, arrests had been thwarted.

Law in Nevada was haphazard. Those remote outposts that did boast a sheriff were scattered far and wide across the barren terrain. Thus far it had given the gang no problems.

One of the most resolute was Sheriff Gabe Pershing of Winnemucca. He would have liked nothing more than to bring the culprits to justice. A staunch servant of the law, he controlled the most difficult part of the territory. However, extensive ranges of mountains criss-crossing the terrain made pursuit of felons well nigh impossible. And without a co-ordinated force of deputies, he had little chance of running the gang to earth.

Following yet another frustrating report from an aggrieved stagecoach operator, it was Pershing who had labelled them the Bloody Blackjacks. The name had stuck, much to the delight of Rafe Culpepper.

His own particular nickname might have been considered an insult by some dudes, but Big-Nose Rafe revelled in the bulbous snout which was a prominent feature of his visage. The name had caught on due to the gang leader's penchant for sniffing out lucrative jobs that earned a good remuneration.

Their current foray was the gang's sixth stage robbery. Continue in this way and the infamous reputation of the Blackjacks would spread far beyond the territorial boundaries of Nevada. The only fly in the ointment had been the shooting of one of the stagecoach passengers. And it was down to the hot-headed gun hand of the youngest gang member.

Kid Syrillo vigorously claimed that he had been given no choice. It was only when they had got well away from the main trail that Culpepper drew the gang to a halt to challenge the Kid.

'Why did you gun down the woman?' he rapped out, skewering the cocky young braggart with an evil eye. 'There's gonna be a right ruckus on account of that, you durned young fool.'

The Kid bristled but knew better than to argue the point. He composed his youthful features before answering. Long straw locks straggled from beneath his flat-crowned hat. It was a look in keeping with the Kid's idol. Syrillo was only a nipper when he had witnessed the legendary showdown between James Butler Hickok, known throughout the West as Wild Bill, and Dave Tutt back in 1865. The two men had argued over a card game in the Old Lyon saloon in the Missouri town of Springfield. Tutt had nonchalantly picked up Hickok's pocket watch from the table and walked off with it.

In the public square later that day, he challenged Hickok to take it back. In the duel that ensued, Tutt stood no chance against the deadly accuracy of Wild Bill's .36 Navy Colt. Although the incident went to court, Hickok was judged to have fired in self-defence and acquitted.

The respect accorded the renowned gunfighter had stuck with the Kid who resolved to follow in the same path. His chance had come when at the age of sixteen, he had shot down a so-called friend for muscling in on a girl whom Syrillo fancied. The boy died of his wound which set the Kid on a life of crime.

Having drifted west, he joined up with the Blackjacks three years later in 1874.

'I thought she was reaching for a gun in her bag,' he asserted firmly when challenged by Culpepper. 'Just because she was a woman don't mean the dame didn't have sharp claws.'

The leery snigger elicited nods of agreement from some of the others. There were plenty of hellcats in the numerous saloons they had frequented to prove the point. Seeing that he had support, Syrillo added with a brash smirk, 'Anyhow, it sure made all those other passengers easy to deal with.'

Culpepper understood that the young firebrand had reacted instinctively. It was a good quality to have, but needed the experience of an older hand to channel it in the right direction. Although none too pleased with the incident that he himself would have avoided, the gang boss accepted the Kid's explanation. After all, Syrillo was a first-rate gun slick: he just needed that reckless nature taming. And Rafe Culpepper figured he was the man to do it.

Nonetheless, he added a terse postscript to his previous warning. 'Next time, think with your brain, Kid, and not your trigger finger.'

But another member of the gang was not so forgiving.

Cheyenne Brady saw it as a reckless and dangerous act that had put all their lives in danger. Although an owlhoot, Brady hailed from the old school where all woman were accorded iconic status. Shooting one down like that was the action of a coward. He had hinted as much during the ride back to Gabbs Hole.

The tall man had never tried to conceal his Indian heritage. Indeed, he took pride in being the product of a dalliance between a white army officer and the daughter of Chief White Bull of the Northern Cheyenne. Inevitably, the liaison had been doomed from the start. Brady had been removed from the bosom of his tribal home to be raised by his father amidst the traditions of the US cavalry.

But he had never forgotten his heritage.

To the progeny of many similar associations, it was a hindrance throughout life. Cheyenne Brady, however, embraced his half-breed status with gusto. Being granted the advantage of his father's appearance meant that Brady's Indian blood was rarely an issue.

Even so, he adopted the name of his tribe in preference to the American name of Travis chosen by his father. He was also able to absorb the best of both factions. The Indian ability to survive in harsh environments, making use of all that the land had to offer was effectively combined with the white man's organization and superior development in a new world order. These rare attributes were quickly recognized by the military.

Cheyenne Brady became an army scout. Eagle feathers stuck in his hat complemented the buckskin fringed jacket and cemented his appointment.

It proved, however, to be a double-edged sword. Working against his tribal instincts proved too much for the young scout and he went off the rails. Drinking and hallooing in the saloons soon got him into trouble with the military authorities. Languishing in a stockade after one session, he met up with Rafe Culpepper who also recognized the 'breed's unique assets. And it was he who suggested using them in a way that would prove to be far more lucrative than scouting for the army.

With Culpepper's guile and cunning they managed to escape.

And from that day onwards, Cheyenne Travis Brady

rode the owlhooter trail.

Tension between Cheyenne and Kid Syrillo had fes-tered until it was ready to blow as they entered the Hole at sunset. The pair squared off facing each other. Surrounded by the rest of the gang, it was Culpepper who prevented any gunplay by ordering that any disagreement should be sorted out in the time-honoured fashion of a fist fight.

The boss valued both men and did not want to lose either of them.

Unbuckling their gun rigs, the two protagonists settled down in the circle formed by their watching sidekicks. Both opponents had a second to attend them at the end of each five-minute round. Bets were avidly placed on the potential winner of the contest.

A burly dude by the name of Mesa Quinn held all the stake money. He had once been a bank teller so was good with numbers. Handling all that dough in the bank had proved too much of a temptation to Quinn who had decided to skim off some of the takings. The scheme had worked for a couple of months until the auditors from head office cottoned on.

After serving two years on a Texas chain gang, he headed north where his quick brain and inside knowledge of the banking business caught the attention of Rafe Culpepper.

'Any more bets before the fun begins?' enquired Quinn.

'Put me another ten bucks on Brady,' said old Moonshine, handing over his stake.

'No eye-gouging, hair-pulling, or any other form of

cheating. This is gonna be a straight fight wearing these,' Culpepper ordered, throwing a pair of padded leather gloves to each of the contestants. 'I found these in a sporting goods store last time we were in Eureka Springs. This is their first outing. An English guy called the Marquis of Queensberry is reckoned to have invented the rules using them. The loser is the man who gives up first, or fails to stand after a count of ten.'

'What do they call it, boss?' asked an inquisitive weasel who went by the handle of Chinstrap on account of his Shoshone beaded hat adornment.

Culpepper's prominent snout twitched as he gave the enthusiastic onlooker an imperious stare in his capacity as the self-appointed referee. Then he added this final piece of information. 'He calls it boxing. And I reckon its gonna catch on.'

The gang dutifully acknowledged their leader's superior knowledge.

Syrillo snarled at his antagonist. The Kid was impatient, eager to get started.

'Each round starts and stops with a bang on this tin plate. Are you both ready?'

A curt nod from each man and the contest was set in motion.

The brash Kid instantly flung himself at Brady who was caught out by the sudden lunge. The two men went sprawling in the dust. Culpepper scowled. This was not how a proper boxing match was supposed to go according to the book he'd read. Too late to interfere now.

Rolling over and over, each man struggled to come out on top. Fists flew back and forth, but had little power.

Eventually, Brady managed to thrust the lighter man aside. Scrambling to his feet he placed his legs wide apart for balance, fists raised ready for the next assault.

A lurid smile from Culpepper. That was better. Maybe Cheyenne had read the same book.

Once again the Kid made to rush at his opponent. But this time, Brady was ready. As Syrillo blundered in, the 'breed shot two solid punches at his jaw. Each one rattled the Kid's teeth pulling him up short. Taking advantage of the bruising encounter, Brady planted another straight left forcing the Kid back. He stumbled into the outer ring of men who immediately pushed him back towards his opponent. Cheers of encouragement from both sets of supporters echoed around the rocky enclave of Gabbs Hole.

'Watch his left, Kid,' hollered one of the younger outlaws called Elko Boon.

'Go on, Cheyenne,' yelled old Moonshine. 'You can wipe the floor with this young whippersnapper.'

Wildly swinging his arms, Syrillo managed to catch his opponent with a lucky right swing that cracked Brady's left ear. Roars of approval mingling with gasps of dismay greeted the stunning blow. For a moment Brady saw stars before stepping aside out of range as the Kid blundered past. Both men having sustained cuts and bruises, Culpepper chose that moment to hammer on his tin plate bringing the first round to a halt.

'Take a rest, boys,' he said assuming an imperious stance in the middle of the ring. 'And next time I don't want any more brawling on the ground. Let's have a proper boxing match.'

The seconds got to work. Old Moonshine removed a bottle from his knapsack and offered it to Cheyenne. 'That stuff will clear your head in no time, son,' he stressed, at the same time sticking a lighted cheroot into the boxer's mouth. 'It's a fresh brew I've just made.' He wagged a finger when Cheyenne tipped the bottle to his lips. 'Not too much. We don't want you getting blurry-eyed. That young punk ain't no pushover. You need all your wits where a varmint like him is concerned.'

'OK, boys, that's enough. Seconds away.'

A watching buzzard cawed its approval as Culpepper hammered on the plate, and the second round was under way.

This time, both men held back, circling warily around the fight zone waiting for a suitable opening. A gaggle of geese passed by overhead. But their honking was drowned out by the spirited support from the Blackjacks. Only Rafe Culpepper remained silent as he studied each man's technique.

His men were eager for more action. One of them pushed Brady from behind. The half-breed stumbled into his opponent. Syrillo immediately took the opportunity of landing a couple of solid jabs before the rest were blocked. Sensing that he was gaining the upper hand, the Kid smirked.

'Feeling your age, redskin?' He knew that Brady hated his Indian heritage being denigrated. It was a deliberate ploy to unsettle the older man. 'The pace getting too hot for you?'

Brady's craggy features remained taciturn. He ignored the taunt, concentrating instead on securing an opening

14

of his own. It came when the Kid started making overconfident feints trying to lure the other man into a fruitless lunge.

Brady waited for the right moment before grabbing hold of the thrusting arm. A quick shift of the hips as he spun on his heel. Then he hurled the stick-thin Kid over his shoulders. Syrillo flew across the open ground forcing the watchers to part. He landed with a heavy thud, the breath driven from his body.

The plate banged as Culpepper brought the round to a stop.

'We were only halfway through the round,' Moonshine complained forcefully. 'Cheyenne had him beat.'

'I don't want any of that kind of scrapping,' Culpepper shouted, admonishing the illicit move. 'I want to see a boxing match not a bar-room brawl.'

Moonshine responded with a surly shrug. 'This ain't a proper fight. Gloves and banging plates. An American set-to don't need no rules. This Queensberry dude don't know a thing.'

'I'm the one who decides that,' the gang leader spat back. 'You got a beef with that, old-timer?' His hand hovered menacingly above the large Remington Rider on his hip.

'Just saying, is all,' Moonshine grumbled, with a shrug of his bony shoulders.

'Well don't,' rapped Culpepper rubbing his large snout. 'Best thing you can do is see to your man. All this jawing is wasting time.'

Moonshine took the hint. He wiped the caked blood from Brady's mouth, pushing another shot of the strong liquor at him.

It was refused. 'Reckon I'll be better off with some water,' he said. 'Keep my head clear.'

'Well if'n this scrap has to be fought according to them danged rules,' Moonshine muttered under his breath, 'I'll make durned sure that young tearaway keeps to them.'

During the following three rounds, both men sustained punishment. Their faces bore the physical evidence of fist on bone. The gloves prevented any serious injury although it was becoming readily apparent that Brady was gaining the better of his opponent.

The Kid was tiring fast. Huge gulps of air indicated that the pummelling was taking a fierce toll on his stamina. Youthful exhuberance was clearly no match for cunning and a wily approach to the new sport of boxing.

But Kid Syrillo was not finished yet. He was done with all this Queensberry rubbish. It was time to finish the contest, and in his favour no matter what it took.

As soon as the next round began, he palmed a small throwing knife that had been hidden in his boot. Arm raised he was about to launch the deadly blade when a blast of gunfire bounced off the surrounding rock walls.

Culpepper had spotted the sly manoeuvre and responded accordingly. A revolver leapt into his waiting palm and spat flame and hot lead. The Kid cried out as the knife shattered under the slug's impact.

'I said there would be no cheating,' snarled Culpepper, waving the nickel-plated revolver in the culprit's face. 'Weren't you listening to what I said?' He didn't wait for a reply. 'Obviously not. And for that you lose a half share from your proceeds of the robbery. Maybe that'll learn you to take orders in future.'

Syrillo growled under his breath as he nursed his aching hand. He looked to his buddies for support. But there was no sympathy from any of the others. Even Elko Boon threw a scornful look at the trickster. They all enjoyed a good scrap, just so long as it was fair.

By drawing a knife, the Kid had bucked the code and would be shunned until such time as the boss decided he had got the message. The morose outcast shuffled away while the others crowded around Cheyenne Brady slapping him on the back. Everyone likes to be associated with a winner.

'You done well against that young upstart, Cheyenne,' praised Culpepper as the winner buckled on his gunbelt. 'You can have the extra dough the Kid has forfeited.'

Brady nodded his thanks, taking a welcome slug from Moonshine's jug.

Had he noticed the scowling grimace that Kid Syrillo slung in his direction, Brady might not have been so nonchalant. Daggers of hate speared the fight winner's back as Syrillo slunk away. The young tearaway was not about to forgive and forget the humiliation he had suffered at the half-breed's hands.

TWO

REVENGE

Rafe Culpepper peered down at his gold pocket watch to check the time.

It was noon and the Blackjacks were secreted within the confines of Emigrant Pass. The narrow gap was the only way through the soaring Cortez and Tuscarora mountain ranges.

The gang leader was particularly proud of the time-piece. He had acquired it from the territorial governor during the gang's previous robbery of the Ruth copper-mine payroll. Perry Langhorn had been campaigning to get himself elected to the prestigious job. He figured it would be in his best interest to take the regular stagecoach thus advertising his credentials as a man of the people.

Not a smart move.

Unfortunately for him and the rest of the passengers, that particular run had been targeted by the Blackjacks. And it was no ordinary run. The stage was also carrying a substantial transfer of funds between the banks of Virginia City and Winnemucca.

Had the aspiring governor not voiced his objections to the heist, he might have been left alone. But Langhorn wanted to appear as the champion of law and order. As a result, he had been stripped down to his long johns much to the hilarity of the outlaws. The rest of his goods had also been appropriated. The amusing sight of the defrocked official did not amuse the other passengers who had their own valuables appropriated.

Chinstrap had taken a particular liking to the bank manager's beaverskin hat while Syrillo fancied the governor elect's smart silk vest. Inevitably, a whiskey drummer had all his samples taken. As leader, Culpepper secured the main prize which was the gold watch and chain that now adorned his person.

When he reached civilization, Langhorn had voiced his anger at the affront in numerous Nevada news sheets, promising to rid the territory of these odious brigands if he were elected. The ruse had worked. He had won the election. But a year later, the new Governor of Nevada was no nearer to carrying out his election manifesto.

So here they were in the confines of Emigrant Pass awaiting the arrival of their next heist.

'Check your hardware, boys,' Culpepper breezed with a grim smile. 'That troop of blue bellies should be entering the Pass any time now.'

They were waiting for the arrival of a contingent of the 3rd Nevada Horse. Since their wages had been lifted from the regular stagecoach, the colonel in charge of Fort Lovelock had decreed that all further payroll shipments should have an armed escort.

This was where the superior knowledge of Cheyenne Brady came into play.

He was personally acquainted with one of the clerks who worked in the payroll office. Over a few drinks in the Comstock saloon in Virginia City, Brady had plied the guy with free drinks. He had soon learned that Corporal Henry Hegerty was in debt to the tune of one hundred dollars to a local gambler.

The clerk had no hope of repaying the debt and the tinhorn was threatening to inform the army authorities. Such a disclosure would mean Hegerty being busted back to private and losing his cushy job, not to mention serving a spell in the stockade.

Brady had the perfect solution to his problem.

So it was arranged that Hegerty would persuade the colonel to send the next payroll shipment by a more obscure route to avoid any potential threat. The route of the old California Trail was chosen. During the 1840s it had been a major highway for settlers and gold prospectors travelling to California. Thousands of wagons had passed this way over the years; their rutted course could still be seen. But the traffic had tailed off in recent times having been superceded by the trans-continental railroads.

The ex-scout knew that Colonel Cosgrave was a stickler for protocol. Everything was done by the book. So he would expect his men to be rigidly attired in full uniform and riding in a strict two-by-two formation. There would be no more than eight men together with a junior officer assigned to the patrol. And Hegerty had assured the gang that the payroll would be in the saddle-bags of the two central riders, one of whom would be himself. The army clerk had decided to go the whole hog and join up with the Blackjacks. In truth, he did not fancy his chances of escaping justice once the military investigation team got to work. And why accept a miserly hundred bucks for his trouble when he could command a much larger stake?

Big-Nose Rafe was none too pleased at being dictated to by some hick bluecoat. But he went along with the plan. Hegerty had assured his contact that the payroll would be in excess of 5,000 lovely greenbacks. The army man had no difficulty getting himself assigned to the patrol. Planning for such a heist was, therefore, child's play.

All the gang needed to do was catch the patrol in a restricted enclave where movement was limited. Emigrant Pass offered the perfect spot to effect a successful ambush.

Culpepper had positioned his men on both sides of the Pass. His narrowed gaze was fixed on a point towards the entrance of the ravine. From there, Chinstrap would signal when the patrol was sighted. The idea was to allow the bluecoats to get well into the constricted gap giving them little opportunity to manoeuvre.

Hegerty had told Brady that he would be wearing a black arm band. Ostensibly it was in memory of a deceased relative. In fact, the band was to identify him to the gang thus preventing him being shot down once the action started.

A gloomy band of grey cloud blotted out the heat of the noonday sun. A portent of things to come perhaps. But for whom?

A beaded beaverskin hat waved from down near the

entrance to the Pass. That was the signal from Chinstrap that the troopers were approaching.

Backs stiffened.

Any minute now and the patrol would come into view. Culpepper had given orders not to open fire until a challenge to halt and surrender the dough had been issued. He was confident that the challenge would be ignored. And if such was the case, nobody was to be spared, except of course, the Judas in their midst.

The gang boss had other plans for him.

Once the patrol had passed beneath where Chinstrap and another gang member called Jackknife Stringer were positioned, these two front runners then dropped down on to the trail behind some boulders to effectively block off any retreat.

Culpepper grinned. The precision tactic had come straight out of a military officer's handbook; one that Cheyenne Brady had purloined.

Seconds later the patrol trotted into view.

The lieutenant in front would be the first to go down once the shooting started. Cut off the head and the rest of the body would quickly wither. Culpepper stood up. But he made sure that he was concealed behind a clump of beavertail cacti.

'That's far enough, soldier boys,' he called out in a gruff voice that effectively carried in the confined space of the Pass. 'You have some dough that needs transferring to us.'

Taken completely off-guard, the young officer instinctively obeyed. His face registered dazed surprise before the stunning import of the order sank in. Then his military training took over. Drawing his cavalry sword in a

22

futile gesture of disregard, he dug his spurs into the white horse's flanks and yelled for his men to charge down the narrow trail.

That was the signal for all hell to break loose.

Guns opened fire from both sides of Emigrant Pass. The young officer was punched off his horse, dead before his bullet-riddled body hit the ground. The remaining troopers bunched up unsure how to respond. Another went down in the mêlée.

Unable to see their antagonists and deprived of leadership, the other bluecoats milled around firing haphazardly. But with no obvious targets, they were doomed to failure. The withering hail of lead rapidly chopped them down.

Two older hands bringing up the rear were made of sterner stuff. Drawing their Springfield rifles they leapt off their horses into cover. The duo succeeded in getting off a few shots. In the meantime. Hegerty had joined in the ambush by shooting down his partner who was toting the other half of the payroll.

This was the chance for which Kid Syrillo had been waiting. Ignoring the others whose entire attention was focused on the gun battle, he sought out the odious form of Cheyenne Brady. A grim smile cracked the Kid's face as he aimed his rifle at the 'breed's head.

Brady went down, shot from behind by one of his own men.

A quick look around to ensure that his treachery had passed unnoticed, Syrillo then rejoined the main affray.

The two remaining troopers were putting up a solid resistance. They had been trained well. Culpepper could see that winkling them out from that position would entail too much of a risk. He had also noted that the Judas bluecoat had secured the payroll and was sneaking away from the scene of conflict. A strategic retreat was, therefore, called before any of his own men were cut down.

'OK, boys,' he called above the noise of gunfire. 'We have what we came for. Now let's burn some dust.'

Syrillo threw a probing look towards where Cheyenne had fallen behind some rocks. There was no movement from the injured man. The backshooter had done his work well. He sneered at the blooded heap of buckskins. Nobody defiles the name of Kid Syrillo and lives to tell the tale. Then he rejoined his buddies, anxious to get away from Emigrant Pass before Brady was missed. The swirling tendrils of gunsmoke helped in this regard.

'Everybody here?' Culpepper called out.

A brief body count in the hazy smoke-laden atmosphere added up to the correct number. But in the heat of the recent exchange he had failed to realize that although he was one man down, another had joined their ranks.

This omission did not come to light until the gang were well on their way back to Gabbs Hole. A halt was called to check out the loot. That was when Moonshine posed the question that had been niggling him for some time.

'Where's Cheyenne?' he asked. 'Anybody seen him since we left the Pass?'

Puzzled looks were his only replies. The men peered around at each other. But there was no Cheyenne Brady. Having been accepted back into the gang before the payroll snatch, the Kid was eager to add his concern to the baffling enigma.

'Maybe his horse threw a shoe,' he suggested, looking round for agreement.

Culpepper nodded. 'You could be right there, Kid,' he concurred turning to another of his men. 'Jackknife, you ride back a'ways and see if'n you can spot him.'

The lanky rider wrestled his horse around and galloped off.

It was a half-hour before he returned. Alone.

'I rode back as far as that ridge overlooking the Pass. But there was no sign of him.'

That was when Elko Boon voiced the thought uppermost in Culpepper's mind. It was the notion that Syrillo was hoping someone would raise. But not him.

'I reckon he was shot down,' said Boon, 'and we never noticed in all the hullabaloo.'

Culpepper snarled as another thought flashed into his angered brain. He swung to face their newest recruit. 'Maybe it was this critter what done it,' he rasped, pointing his revolver at the gaping trooper. 'They say that a leopard never changes its spots. Just like a double-crossing Judas. You shot him down hoping to grab yourself a bigger share of the loot.'

Culpepper was well into his stride now, convinced that he had solved the mystery. His men were more than eager to accede to their leader's superior acumen. None more so than Kid Syrillo. A set of grim expressions were turned on to the quaking object of their fury.

Hegerty backed away clutching the payroll bags to his chest. The action only served to incense the Blackjacks all the more. The sinewy, mouse-like features contorted as fear gripped the polecat's innards. His guts contracted hard, the gaping mouth filling up with foul-tasting stomach juices.

'It weren't me!' he wailed. 'How could I hope to escape with all this dough?'

It was a perfectly logical claim. But the gang's blood was up. They wanted a reprisal for losing their most popular associate. And who better to provide it than this treacherous varmint. Syrillo was one of the most vehement in his denunciation of the weasel.

Big-Nose Rafe also recalled how he had virtually demanded to join the gang for his help in promoting the robbery. In actual fact it had been a buoyant expectation. But the gang boss had twisted the guy's words to suit his own ends.

'So what's the verdict on this murdering skunk, boys?' hollered Culpepper knowing what the answer would be.

'*Guilty*! *Guilty*!' The strident roar from a myriad of throats echoed across the plains.

Hegerty panicked. He ran across to his horse in a futile effort to escape.

A macabre guffaw erupted from Culpepper's throat. He signalled for one of his men to toss him a rifle. Allowing the Judas to mount up and spur off, he took his time jacking a fresh round into the breech of the Winchester. The gang watched as the fleeing thief attempted to make good his escape.

He had managed over a hundred yards before the gunman casually swung the rifle up to his shoulder and let fly in a single fluid motion. Only the one shot was needed. Hegerty threw up his arms and tumbled from the saddle.

Nobody cheered. Only disdainful scorn was felt for the

26

treacherous runt. Kid Syrillo was the only one who wanted to throw up his arms in triumph. His own treacherous part in the whole sorry affair meant that his nemesis had been effectively dealt with far better than he could ever have expected. But his elation had to be kept under wraps, or he would surely go down the same hellfire trail as the unfortunate bluecoat.

Silently the Blackjacks mounted up and followed their leader as he headed south back to the safety of the Monte Cristos and Gabbs Hole.

THREE

RELEASED

Cheyenne Brady stood outside the territorial prison. Greystoke was well named. A dour menacing presence, its thick stone walls towered over the bleakly austere surroundings five miles to the north of Virginia City. Nothing was allowed to grow within a mile of the penitentiary to maintain its sense of isolation. A grim bastion indeed in which the army scout turned outlaw had spent the last five years.

Brady had kept his head down during the spell of incarceration for his part in the payroll heist at Emigrant Pass. As a result, it had earned him a three year remission off his sentence.

He peered round at the vista beyond the brooding walls. Not that there was anything to see. All his possessions were stuck in a gunnysack which he now hefted over his shoulder before setting out on the walk into town. In his pocket jangled the ten dollars allocated to released prisoners. The idea was for them to buy a ticket out of the territory, never to return.

Four other convicts had been released at the same time as Brady. No transport had been offered by the prison authorities to reach the nearest settlement. So, heads down against the incessant northerly wind, and cocooned in their own thoughts, the sorry-looking quintet set off on the trek to Virginia City.

They were all just glad to have rid themselves of Greystoke's harsh regime.

Brady still wore his old buckskin jacket although it was now much soiled and torn. The eagle feathers in his hat had long since disappeared.

But at least the Colt Frontier had been returned together with its tooled leather rig. He now drew the revolver and twirled the finely balanced handgun on his middle finger. A quick flourish and it disappeared back into the holster. A cheesy grin split the stubbled countenance. At least he still had the dexterity to protect himself should the need arise.

Then a grim expression clouded his face.

Every single day during his term of imprisonment, Brady had pondered over the circumstances that had led to his current situation. The last thing he recalled was drawing a bead on the soldiers after they had refused to surrender the payroll.

But he had been given no chance to open fire. A loud crack, then darkness had enfolded his body in its Stygian embrace.

The next thing he recalled was being hauled to his feet

by one of the surviving troopers.

Sergeant Tug Manson had informed the court at Brady's trial that the patrol had been completely surprised by the ambush. In his considered opinion, none of the bushwhackers had been brought down by his men. Yet he had found one still alive after the attackers had departed with the stolen payroll along with one of his men.

The body of Corporal Hegerty had later been found with a bullet in his back. Manson could only suggest that the trooper had been taken as a hostage in case of pursuit. He must have been shot when the gang had no further need of his services. No mention was made of Hegerty's duplicitous involvement in the robbery. The Judas had taken that piece of information to his grave.

And Brady had not felt it worth declaring the Judas's part seeing as he was now dead. The fact that Rafe Culpepper and the rest of the gang had assumed he had gunned Brady down had clearly not come to light either.

Manson gave his evidence under the watchful eye of Judge Tyrone Lander.

'It was a groaning behind some boulders further up the Pass that attracted my attention, Your Honour,' Manson told the court when the question regarding Brady's discovery was broached. 'Me and Private Jacks crept up on either side of the trail, careful like, just in case some of the critters were waiting to finish us off. But all we found was the accused with a bullet wound scoring his head. Jacks was all for finishing the bastard off.'

A stickler for correct protocol, the judge sniffed. He speared the witness with a malignant glare. Manson quickly got the message.

'Sorry about the language, Your Honour,' he apologized with a bow. 'But with the lieutenant dead, I was left in charge. And I wanted some answers.'

Manson paused to gather his thoughts. The whole court was hushed, waiting for him to continue. Outside, a flash of lightning lit up the gloomy surroundings inside the courthouse. The patter of raindrops could be heard on the roof. A clap of thunder soon followed heralding the start of a thunderstorm. It was an ominous portent of doom that was not lost on the defendant hunched in the dock.

The loud crackle jerked the witness out of his preoccupied melancholia. Resurrecting the grim recollection was not a pleasant experience. The bloody incident had given the tough army sergeant nightmares. He had handled numerous Indian uprisings with composure and self-confidence. But this had been different.

It was the first time he had encountered a heavily armed gang of Americans, even if'n they were outlaws who were intent on wiping out an entire patrol to steal their wages.

'Go on please, Sergeant Manson,' Judge Lander encouraged the ashen-faced trooper. 'I know that reliving the deaths of your comrades is difficult, but it needs to be done. So, take your time.'

Manson coughed before recommencing his monologue. His brow furrowed in puzzlement as he slung a thumb at the prisoner standing despondently in the dock.

'This guy had been shot. But it couldn't have been done by one of my men.'

'How do you arrive at that conclusion, Sergeant?' asked

the prosecuting attorney. Jackson Pike was a cadaverous birdlike man whose beaky nose probed the thick atmosphere like a pecking buzzard.

'The angle of the bullet wound was all wrong,' replied Manson who was now operating on firmer ground. The sergeant did not elaborate.

It was left for the lawyer Pike to impatiently prompt him, 'Go on please. The court is avidly waiting to hear your testimony.'

'The laceration caused by the bullet was across the rear of his head,' Manson explained. 'Such a shot could only have come from behind.'

'What are you implying by this allegation?' asked the lawyer.

'Just to repeat that it sure wasn't one of my men who shot him.'

'Are you, therefore, saying that the accused was shot by one his own men?' The hawkish lawyer's beady eyes lifted in astonishment.

Manson shrugged. 'That ain't for me to say. You're the lawyer. So you work it out.'

'It could have been a stray shot,' piped up a young fresh-faced man who was acting as defence attorney. 'A mistake by one of his comrades. But the main point is this' – Hyram Gandy paused for effect, waiting for complete silence before delivering his masterstroke – 'Sergeant Manson's testimony proves that my client could not have participated in the murder of the patrol as he was already *hors de combat*. He cannot accordingly be guilty of homicide.'

Murmuring erupted from the gallery of the courtroom

as onlookers digested this unusual development in the case.

The verdict imposed by the twelve good men and true of the jury was never in doubt. Cheyenne Brady was found guilty of highway robbery. But in view of Sergeant Manson's surprising piece of evidence, Judge Lander reduced the sentence he had expected to impose.

How the accused had come to be shot did not remain a mystery for long. As far as Cheyenne was concerned it stuck out a mile; just like Rafe Culpepper's snout. Kid Syrillo had tried to kill him. And the skunk had taken the coward's way with a bullet from behind. It was lucky for Cheyenne that the Kid had not checked the accuracy of his shot.

There was only one way of dealing with a lowlife of Syrillo's ilk. Fists bunched in anger as the whole sorry episode was relived, his prison-grey features were soured by a frowning grimace as the ex-convict figured out how best to tackle the thorny issue.

An old guy was plodding along beside him. Brady hadn't noticed the old timer, so intent was he on convincing himself that it was Kid Syrillo who had gunned him down. There was no proof, but all the signs pointed that way.

'Got any plans, Cheyenne?' The enquiry came from a grizzled veteran of the prison system.

Sourdough Lamar had been a gold prospector during the '59 Comstock rush. He had shot his partner claiming the skunk had tried to steal his poke. The jury had not believed him, instead shifting the blame on to Lamar's shoulders. Like most convicts, Soughdough had always vigorously proclaimed his innocence.

It didn't matter now. He was free. And another strike was likely waiting just around the next bend for an enterprising jasper like him. The old guy was an eternal optimist which is what had sustained him during his long spell in the pen. Had he brooded on being falsely convicted, Sourdough would have long since headed for that glorious *El Dorado* in the sky.

Cheyenne eyeballed the old greybeard. A wily gleam sparkled in his blue eyes. Sourdough had become like the grim bastion he had so recently left. Grey and pallid. What Brady did not realize was that he looked no different.

'Just wondering if'n we might be heading in the same direction, is all,' the old guy added with a nonchalant shrug. 'We both have the chance of a fresh start.'

Brady considered the remark, mulling over his options.

He could let his vengeful thoughts over Kid Syrillo fester and eat him alive. Or he could put the past behind him and, like Lamar said, start afresh. The term in Greystoke had been a brutal experience not to be repeated. But at least it had given him a clean sheet. Now he had the chance to begin a new life without having to worry about getting chased by posses. Living the life of the owlhooter in grubby remote hideouts no longer held an attraction.

A new beginning. It was an uplifting prospect.

'Reckon I'll head up to Winnemucca on the Humboldt,' he murmured following the period of reflection.

'You got kin up there?' asked Lamar his bleary gaze focused on a small herd of deer crossing their trail up ahead.

34

Brady's eyes filled up. 'My pa passed on while I was inside.'

The comment was flat, devoid of emotion. But the pain was there etched across the coarse features for the old-timer to see. Lamar kept silent. This was no time for idle chitchat. The two men continued along the trail. It was Brady who eventually broke the silence.

'He started up a blacksmithing business after retiring from the army. A lawyer told me it had been closed after Pa died, but it would be mine when I got out of jail. If'n I didn't want the place, he offered to act as a broker in the sale.' Brady's gaze also followed the string of deer as they picked a course through the clutter of sagebrush and juniper. 'Reckon I'll try and make a go of it. We lost touch after I turned outlaw. I'm just glad that he never learned the truth. Maybe now I'll have the chance to make up for lost time.'

'You ever done that kinda work, boy?' posited Sourdough. There was a hint of cynicism in the comment. 'It's a tough business.'

Brady shook his head.

'Then perhaps you might consider me coming in as a partner.'

The offer elicited a sceptical frown as the old prospector hurried on. 'I learned the trade in Bluetail Gulch over in the Dakota Black Hills. My claim wasn't paying out so I teamed up with a Swede called Big Daddy. That guy had muscles where he should have had ears.' Cheyenne suppressed a smile. 'And he sure knew about smithing. Taught me all the basics.' He shot Brady a hopeful look. 'So what about it? Before doing my time in Greystoke, I banked a hefty slice of paydirt from the Aurora strike. So I got the readies to make it a going concern.'

The old guy was fair jumping with enthusiasm.

But Cheyenne Brady was a level-headed dude. It was a trait inherited from his Indian mother. He never jumped into a creek without testing the water first. So it was only when they were approaching the outskirts of Virginia City that he finally made up his mind.

'It's been three years since Pa died. Like as not I'll need new equipment,' he said, staring ahead at the burgeoning township. 'And enough to do the place up. You ready to fork out to put the place back in business?'

'I ain't offering out the goodness of my heart, young fella,' rapped the old timer. 'I'll want an equal return on the profits.'

'It'll sure beat going after a loan from the bank,' muttered Cheyenne. His thick eyebrows lifted as another thought struck home. 'That is if'n they'd even consider granting a loan to an ex-jailbird.' He held out his hand. 'You got yourself a deal . . . partner.'

Sourdough's grin was wider than the Rio Grande. He extracted one of his silver dollars and flicked it into the air.

'Then let's seal our agreement in time-honoured fashion over a few drinks.'

There was no shortage of drinking dens along Virginia City's main drag. Names such as the Comstock, Miner's Haven, Long Tom and Golden Horseshoe were all vying for the lucrative trade of those who had gold burning a hole in their pockets. The most obvious choice as far as the two partners were concerned was the Lucky Strike.

They pushed through the batwings into a dense fug of

tobacco smoke and beer fumes.

Sourdough paused inside the gloomy den. He breathed deep.

'Don't that taste and smell like pure nectar,' he wheezed, eyes shut tight. Cheyenne coughed. His description of the heady atmosphere would have turned the air bright blue. But he held his peace allowing Lamar to order a bottle of best Scotch. The old guy waited his turn at the bar while a couple of prospectors were having their dust weighed by the bartender.

A wistful expression creased the leathery features. It was just like old times.

'You boys struck it rich?' he enquired, casually thinking back to his own past experiences. A rose-tinted image filtered out all the bad times. The Aurora strike up near Pyramid Lake had been the best. Nuggets the size of duck eggs had been there for the taking. Luckily he'd managed to cash them in before that double-dealing skunk Crusty McCoy had overturned the apple cart.

'What's it to you, mister?' rasped a gravel-cracked voice. A thick ginger beard twitched revealing broken teeth yellowed from baccy chewing. 'Figuring to muscle in on our success, are you?'

'Just a friendly enquiry,' countered the bewildered ex-con.

'Ugh!' snarled redbeard's equally hirsute buddy. But this one had a patch over one eye. His good one offered a menacing glare to the grizzled veteran. 'We've heard that excuse before. Next thing we knew after leaving the saloon, some thieving skunks attacked us and stole our catch.'

'Like as not, you plan to do the same,' snarled redbeard 'Well you and your buddies ain't gonna get the chance.'

The two men backed off. Redbeard flicked his coat aside to reveal a holstered revolver. Lamar was stunned. And his reactions were slow. He just stood there, anchored to the spot.

Redbeard went to draw his pistol. The gun lifted, a grubby thumb dragging back the hammer of a silver .36 Manhattan five shot.

Cheyenne was sitting back in his seat revelling in the joy of freedom. There was much to celebrate: being released from the pen, not to mention a new beginning. Yes indeed, life was sure looking hunky dory.

Then the raised voices at the bar butted in on his dreamy thoughts. A trenchant look across the room managed to penetrate the yellow haze. He picked out the source of the fracas and was just in time to see a large jasper going for his pistol.

And old Sourdough was the target.

Pure instinct clicked in. A blur of speed and his own gun was palmed. No fancy twirling this time. An orange tongue of flame leapt from the barrel. Redbeard staggered back clutching at his shoulder. He banged into his partner and both men went down.

So quick had the incident flared up that none of the other customers was given time to react. They all stared at the two protagonists, mouths gaping wide with shock. Some were still clutching raised glasses in their hands. Others had paused in their game of poker. A tableau frozen in time. The silence that followed was eerie with menace.

Cheyenne was the first to speak. His harsh mandate was for the surviving miner. It was terse, hissing out like a rattler's tongue. 'You ready to take over from your partner?' He had deliberately aimed high to prevent a killing shot. Redbeard emitted a painful groan.

The other man raised his hands. 'Don't shoot, mister. I ain't carrying a piece.' Gingerly he lowered a hand and pulled aside his coat.

'What was that all about?'

The brusque query from Brady demanded an immediate response.

'Jubal here' – a thumb indicated the injured carrot top – 'got it into his thick head that the old guy was after our poke. Guess he made a mistake.'

'Durned right he did,' Cheyenne hit back, 'and he paid for it too. So I suggest you get this gun-happy jigger to a sawbones before he bleeds to death.' The ex-owlhoot kept his revolver steady as a rock as he snapped out, 'And make certain to get your facts right in future.'

'S-sure thing, mister,' stuttered the other guy staring down the smoking barrel of Cheyenne's gun as he helped his buddy to his feet. 'We'll do that.'

A hawkish eye pursued the two prospectors as they left the saloon. Only then did Brady relax. So too did the other customers. Wary glances were cast towards the buck-skinned stalwart as they avidly discussed the sudden flare-up amongst themselves. Such incidents were not unusual in a mining enclave like Virginia City, but when blood was spilled, it always made for an exciting topic of conversation.

The bartender also heaved a sigh of relief that no

damage had been done.

The last occasion a gunfight had erupted on his premises resulted in him having to fork out for a new back mirror. Such items had to be brought in from the nearest supplier which was in Denver, Colorado. If the participants had been celebrating a good strike, there was no problem with payment for the damage caused, otherwise, the cost had to be borne by the owner even if the culprits were found guilty of affray.

Sourdough was also thanking his lucky stars to be still on his feet. The incident had come and gone in the flick of a eyelash. Only the acrid reek of cordite hanging in the fetid air told of the recent gunplay.

The welcome reprieve from heading to the happy hunting grounds produced a popular result.

Hooking out five of the remaining silver dollars from his pocket, Lamar slammed them down on the counter. 'Everybody up to the bar,' he called out. 'The drinks are on me.'

No second bidding was needed by the customers.

The scraping of chairs was followed by a wild stampede for the bar. Sourdough was immediately surrounded by men who recognized a kindred spirit in their midst. The reason for the celebration was forgotten as men downed the free drinks on offer. Jovial back slapping and toasts to their generous benefactor brought a smile to Brady's face.

He sat back in his seat sipping the Scotch while his new partner wallowed in the unaccustomed attention he was receiving. The old guy deserved his short-lived period of fame. Once they reached Winnemucca, the hard work would really begin. Brady could only hope that his previous reputation would be well and truly buried.

FOUR

NEW BEGINNINGS

It was a week later when the two partners rode down the main street of Winnemucca. They had been forced to take some casual work in a wood yard to raise enough dough for the journey north.

Brady's eyes flicked from side to side searching for the premises he had been left in his father's will. Like all miners, old Sourdough was instinctively drawn to the most garish and lively saloon. The Midas Touch rang all the right bells. And it had the appropriate name.

'Reckon we're gonna do well in this joint, boy,' he breezed, easing his mount over to the nearest hitching rail. 'How's about we celebrate with a few drinks?'

But Cheyenne had other ideas.

'Not until we've checked out the place I've inherited.' His firm decline drew a scowl from his buddy. 'The time to celebrate is when we make our first deposit in the bank. Then we'll have earned it. Until then, all your funds ought to be for building up the business.' He aimed a challenging look at Lamar, tempering it with a wry grin.

The old guy knew he was right. 'Old habits are hard to shuck,' he said with a sheepish sigh of regret, eyeballing the saloon with longing as they passed it by. Many's the time that a hard-earned poke had disappeared down his dry throat leaving him broke and full of regrets, only to do exactly the same thing the next time Lady Luck came a-calling.

A lone dog paused midway across the street to peer at the newcomers. It growled before slinking away. It was not the only one to take heed of the two arrivals. Strangers always drew attention in Winnemucca. Numerous eyes followed them down the broad thoroughfare.

They soon located the blacksmith's shop. It was set back off the street. The fencing that enclosed a small corral was broken. And from the outside the place looked derelict. Paint was peeling from the boarded-up front doors; a couple of the windows were broken. It was not a promising introduction for Cheyenne Brady to his new home.

But this was what his father had left him, clearly with the intention that it would make an honest man out of his half-breed son. Cheyenne stiffened his resolve. He was determined not to tarnish his father's memory. Enquiring from a passing cowboy, he learnt that the land agent had an office down a side street some three blocks north. Leaving Sourdough to kick his heels, he went off to claim his inheritance.

After proving his identity, Brady secured the keys from the agent who signed over the deeds. He then led his mount back down the main street to open up and inspect the new holding at close quarters.

More hidden eyes followed his progress. The identity of the newcomer had spread like wildfire. Most of the looks were hostile. It was no secret to whom Colonel Mortimer Brady had left his holding. Having an ex-jailbird living in their community was decidedly worrying.

The reputation of the Blackjacks was known throughout Nevada. Winnemucca had so far escaped their depredations, but how long would that last with Cheyenne Brady in their midst?

Oblivious to the adverse mood he had engendered, Cheyenne tied off to a rotting gate post. The doors grated alarmingly when they were unlocked. If anything, the interior proved to be in worse repair than they had feared. Birds had made themselves at home by gaining access through a hole in the roof. Everything was coated in a thick layer of dust.

A nausea-inducing series of squeaks drew their attention to a corner where a family of rats had settled. Red eyes watched the invaders of their territory.

'First off we're gonna need a dog to root out that vermin,' observed Sourdough ruefully. A shiver ran down his spine. 'Just thinking about them critters gives me the willies.'

Brady examined the ironware lined up beside the firebox. 'At least these things look in good condition,' he remarked, trying to lift the depressed air that had settled over the new occupants. 'They just need cleaning up.'

A harsh cough sounded behind them. Both men swung to face their first visitor. A dark shadow filled the doorway. But what caught both men's attention was the silver star pinned to his tan vest. Brady sighed. Not the visitor he would have wished for on his first day in town. It sure hadn't taken long for the vultures to gather.

The man was dressed in a smart black suit and hat beneath which sat a handlebar moustache waxed at the ends. Sheriff Gabe Pershing had clearly seen newspaper pictures of another renowned law officer who was making a name for himself as a town tamer in Kansas. Cheyenne couldn't resist a smile. He had read the same paper. The lawdog clearly hoped to emulate the success in Winnemucca that Wyatt Earp had achieved in Dodge City.

'You fellas planning on settling down here?' Pershing said in a gruff voice, while trying to effect a casual stance. The query was expressed in a distinctly frigid tone.

'That's the idea, Sheriff,' replied Brady, making an equally forthright declaration. 'Any reason why we shouldn't?'

'Not unless you break the law there isn't.'

'And why should we want to do that?' Brady knew what the lawman was insinuating and it rankled. 'Neither of us is wanted for any crime in this territory or any other.'

'I know who you are, mister,' rasped Pershing. The gloves were off. No more hopping from one foot to the other evading the issue. 'This is a quiet town and we don't want trouble. When other folks learn of your arrival, they are going to be upset that Cheyenne Brady, infamous member of the Bloody Blackjacks, has chosen to settle in their midst.'

Pershing sneered when he saw the newcomer's startled expression.

'Surely you didn't figure to sneak in here as if nothing

had happened,' the lawman answered, embellishing his rejoinder with a thick layer of sarcasm. 'Folks round here respected your pa, but the same sure don't go for his half-breed offspring.' Pershing fingered his revolver.

Brady stiffened. The situation was becoming decidedly tense.

A small crowd had gathered behind the lawman. It appeared that the identity of the new arrivals had indeed travelled, and much faster than he had expected. They were all eager to observe the outcome of the confrontation.

'You aiming to use that hogleg, Sheriff?' countered Cheyenne, keeping his hands well clear of his own hardware.

Pershing was given no chance to reply as a short plump man pushed his way to the forefront of the restive group.

'What are you doing chinwagging with this man, Sheriff?' snapped the imperious intruder. Judging by his natty attire, he was somebody of substance in the community. 'We don't want his kind in Winnemucca. You should be ordering him to leave right now.' Murmurs of approval greeted the blunt demand made by Amos Wendover, the Mayor of Winnemucca.

'Now then, Amos, we can't be too hasty,' replied Pershing, trying to retain control of the situation. 'As long as these guys do not break the law, they have every right to remain. Vigilante law has no place in Winnemucca. And anybody who tries it will have me to face.' The lawman backed up his threat with a withering scowl.

'But he's a known criminal, a Bloody Blackjack that you youself have denounced,' Wendover persisted. The mayor was keen to raise his own standing in the community. And he was not a man to be thwarted in his mission of extradition. 'Even now his gang could be watching the town, just waiting for the signal to invade us.'

The crowd shuffled restively.

'The mayor is right,' agreed Norbert Dench who ran the general store. 'We need to think about the safety of our kinfolks.'

Brady had heard enough. This was getting out of hand. Another few minutes and they would both be run out of town on a rail. He needed to establish his own credentials before it was too late.

'Me and my partner have paid our dues to society,' he pressed stepping forward. 'Sure, I was a road agent. But that's in the past. Now I want a fresh start. This business was left to me and I want to make a go of it.' Squaring his shoulders, a steely look scanned the hostile gathering. 'And I don't intend to let anyone stop me.'

'We already have a blacksmith,' warbled a thin reedy voice from the back.

Another hawked out a sardonic grunt of disdain. 'You call Mexican Joe a blacksmith? He couldn't change his hairstyle, let alone a set of horseshoes.'

'That's cos he's bald,' cackled a third citizen.

Hearty guffaws greeted this ribald comment. The hostility of the crowd was beginning to thaw, much to Cheyenne's relief. An emphatic rebuttal of his old ways appeared to have hit home. At least some of the crowd felt that on the surface this guy did not appear to pose a threat. And neither did his grizzled old buddy.

The sheriff appeared to concur with the new mood.

'There is nothing wrong with a bit of competition,' he said. Then, once again addressing the two newcomers he added, 'But I'll be keeping a close eye on you two. Any suspicious moves and you'll be thrown out of town.'

The two men held each other's gaze. It was Cheyenne who eased the tension by holding out a hand. 'You got yourself a deal, Sheriff. If'n we put a foot wrong, you can tar and feather the both of us.'

'You speak for yourself, boy,' chipped in a huffy Sourdough Lamar, 'I ain't ready to go to no fancy dress ball clad in a chicken suit.'

More laughs followed as the lawman urged the crowd to disperse. 'OK, folks, the fun's over,' he muttered gently ushering them away. 'Let these fellas get on with their business and we'll not hinder them as long as they abide by the law.'

But the mayor was not finished. He and his friends stood their ground. Wendover turned back for one final snipe at the reformed outlaw. 'You ain't heard the last of this, Brady,' he rapped. 'Not everyone in Winnemucca is as accommodating as our good sheriff here.'

Pershing scowled. His shoulders stiffened. 'The council might pay my wages, but they don't tell me how to run this town. Not until the election anyway. And that ain't until next year. So haul in your hocks, mister, and get about your own affairs.'

'You tell him, Sheriff,' piped up a lone female voice in the crowd. 'I say we let bygones be bygones and not hold grudges. Everyone should be given a second chance in life.'

The speaker pushed her way through to the front of the

crowd. Jody Dunstan was not a woman easily ignored. Her auburn tresses floated gently in the languid breeze framing alabaster features that could have graced a society magazine. Hands resting nonchalantly on shapely hips commanded attention.

A limpid smile mesmerized the object of her declaration. Cheyenne Brady was stunned into silence along with the rest of the onlookers. Theirs was due to the respect in which she was clearly held by the community as the daughter of Josiah Dunstan, the bank manager. The ex-Blackjack was stumped for words. Like a panting bloodhound his tongue was almost hanging out of an open mouth.

He was not the first man to be enthralled by this beauteous creature. Many had plighted their troth. Yet so far Jody Dunstan had shunned them all. And at the grand age of twenty-five she was still single and fancy free.

Nobody moved. All eyes were fastened on to the sassy female. Her gently swaying hips were like the hypnotic allure of a swaying diamondback.

'Well?' snapped the siren, clapping her hands gleefully. 'You guys heard the sheriff. Ain't you all got businesses to run, just like these two gentlemen?' A brief flick of the head indicated the new blacksmiths. The hard western burr had been acquired while living at Fort Belmont when her father was a humble teller in the bank there. It belied the slender genteel persona making her piece of bravado all the more dynamic.

The crowd quickly broke up. Even the mayor and his cronies were nonplussed. Within less than a minute, only the woman and her two new associates were left standing in front of the run-down smithy. Sourdough could see the effect that the woman was having on his partner. A discretionary withdrawal was called for.

'I'll go check out what we need for cleaning up this place,' he announced.

No answer was forthcoming. It appeared that both were equally smitten with each other. The old-timer's visage creased in a knowing smile. Past occasions when he also had been in thrall of female wiles floated dreamily across his mind. He sighed emitting a heartfelt murmur of regret. It was all such a long time ago. A flight of meadowlarks twittering overhead went unnoticed as the old timer sauntered off.

FIVE

A SHOCK FOR CHEYENNE

The next few weeks passed in a flurry of activity. With only a drunk Mexican in competition, the new smithing business took off with alacrity. Jody's association with the local ranching community came in very handy. She even managed to negotiate lucrative contracts for shoeing horses with the main outfits.

Sourdough also proved his worth by teaching his partner the basics of bending and shaping heated steel. Brady was an adept pupil who soon picked up the necessary skills.

It was hard, sweaty work. But both men had never been happier. Cheyenne in particular was cockahoop that Jody Dunstan had chosen to take such an interest in his affairs. Thus far, their relationship had remained friendly and businesslike. Any romantic notions had been deliberately sidetracked. Although Sourdough had no doubts that the latter would eventually come to fruition.

The young woman's father, however, was a different proposition altogether.

Josiah Dunstan was distinctly frosty about the fact that his only daughter was consorting with an ex-jailbird. More important was the man's link with a known outlaw band which was still active in the territory.

It mattered little to the bank manager that Brady claimed to have shunned his owlhooter ways. Dunstan was not convinced. As far as he was concerned, mud sticks. Although he had been forced to concede that so far, the guy appeared to be sticking to his assertion. However, that did not change the banker's view that his daughter should keep her distance.

Thus far, unfortunately, no amount of threats nor pleas for Jody to desist from her involvement with the man had worked. Dunstan was in a quandary. But short of imprisoning his daughter, there was nothing he could do except pray that it was merely a passing whim occasioned by the fellow's previous notoriety.

'I don't want any kin of mine throwing herself at a criminal,' was the constant grumble from the bank manager. 'There are many other more suitable paramours in Winnemucca who would be only too pleased to walk out with you. What about the mayor for instance?'

Jody grimaced at mention of the repellent official. 'I wouldn't give that oily toad the steam off my coffee. Cheyenne has served his time and assures me that he has reformed,' she retorted stiffly. 'And who I choose to associate with is my affair. I'm not a child any longer. So you have no business trying to control my life.'

Her father huffed and puffed, sometimes resorting to threats which always fell on deaf ears. At other times he would try more conciliatory appeals to her common sense.

'By associating with such a man, you are damaging the business that I have built up,' he petitioned her one morning when she called at the office.

Jody's perky nose twitched in disdain as she peered through the window into the public foyer of the bank. 'There certainly doesn't appear to be any shortage of customers. Indeed, I would say that business is positively booming.'

Josiah Dunstan had no answer to that. So he tried another tack.

'And let us hope that it stays that way,' he bristled indignantly. 'These people using our facilities are what keeps you in those fine clothes you are always ordering from the catalogues.'

But it was all to no avail. The suspicious attitude displayed by the rest of the town had moderated considerably. They were impressed by the hard work that Cheyenne and his partner were putting into the business. Perhaps after all he really did intend to go straight. All the signs were certainly pointing in that direction. And so after two months of gruelling labour, Cheyenne was ready to make his first deposit at the bank.

Sourdough had been quick to remind his partner of the promise made all those weeks before.

'Don't forget what we agreed, old buddy,' he prompted as his partner made to leave the smithy. 'We celebrate our success in time-honoured fashion at the Midas Touch.'

'Can't wait.' Cheyenne's wide grin matched the toothy grimace of his partner.

After adjusting his new suit and tie, both of which felt somewhat constricting, he set his hat straight and marched purposefully across the street. The hundred dollar deposit was clutched firmly in his hand as he entered the hallowed premises of the Nevada Central Reserve – Winnemuuca Branch. Ruddy cheeks were positively glowing with pride.

It so happened that Jody had been made aware of the blacksmith's visit. She made sure to be in the office when he arrived.

Her father was going on as usual urging her to find a more suitable male companion.

Jody was enjoying the older man's grousing. She knew that her father only had her best interests at heart, even if they were contrary to her own. The wry smirk accompanied by a wicked twinkle in her eye brought the banker's mouthings stumbling to a halt.

'Why do I sense that you're playing with me, Jody?' he said, trying to inject some starch into the query, and failing miserably. 'You're up to something.'

'Why not look through the window and see,' she breezed, waving a languid hand towards the outer office.

A puzzled frown furrowed her father's brow as he rose and wandered over to the window.

'If you look in your appointments diary, you will see that Cheyenne Brady is booked in for ten o'clock.' They both peered at the wall clock. 'And, like all good businessmen, he is a few minutes early.' The young woman aimed a smile at the new customer through the window before waltzing over to the back door. 'I will leave you now, Father, to give him that warm welcome for which you are so renowned.'

The mocking tone went over the older man's bald pate. Jody accorded him her brightest smile as she left the gaping bank manager stuttering incoherently. Leaving by way of the rear exit, she took a seat in front of the saddle shop to await her paramour's return.

After gathering his thoughts, Josiah Dunstan stepped briskly into the main office.

His next appointment was feeling rather nervous. Not only was this a business transaction, it was also a meeting with the father of the woman with whom Cheyenne Brady was rapidly falling in love.

Pasting a fixed smile on to his round face, Dunstan greeted his new client. Cheyenne's attention was focused on making a good impression both from a business and personal standpoint. They shook hands.

'And what can I do for you, sir?' enquired the banker, struggling to conceal his animosity. But business was business, and not to be refused because of any private reservations. So the shallow smile remained. A detached approach was called for under such circumstances.

'I wish to open a new account and make a deposit of one hundred dollars,' replied the new blacksmith, oblivious to the hidden feelings of the other man. He pushed the wad of notes forward. 'I trust that will be in order?'

The manager was now in full banking mode as his commercial proficiency took over.

'It certainly is, Mr Brady,' gushed the banker rubbing his hands. 'And may I say how pleased I am that your newly established enterprise is going so well.'

And thus the procedure for signing up a new client got under way. Everything was going as usual. Josiah Dunstan's manner had softened towards his amiable new account holder. The conversation was relaxed and less formal as the relevant forms were completed. The banker handed his new client a cigar. It was the finest Havana had to offer and tasted good.

That was when Cheyenne happened to glance in the mirror hanging on the opposite wall. His tanned features turned a paler shade of grey at what he had just seen.

Chilling ripples of trepidation raced down his spine.

Dunstan was prattling on, oblivious to his client's sudden look of anxiety. Cheyenne rubbed his eyes and looked again through the mirror. No, they had not played him false.

Filling out a form behind him was none other than one of his old sidekicks. What in tarnation was Mesa Quinn doing in Winnemucca?

There could be only one reason why the outlaw was visiting the town's bank. The Blackjacks were planning a robbery. Big-Nose Rafe had sent the hard-nosed ex-teller to suss out the place. He must be planning a raid in the not too distant future. And knowing Rafe as he did, it would be within the next few days.

His hand dropped to the gun on his hip. But it was not there. Hardware and business do not mix. Cheyenne had left his revolver back in his quarters at the rear of the smithy. The fact that it might be needed during his meeting at the bank was as far removed from reality as a Chinaman becoming territorial governor.

With Mesa Quinn sporting a twin rigged gunbelt, he could not risk a confrontation in which innocent people might be shot down. So his mouth remained tight shut.

When Cheyenne was released from the territorial prison at Greystoke, he had every intention of going after Kid Syrillo and exacting a terminal revenge for the skunk's treachery. He had no idea that the Kid had acted on his own. And, as far as the gang knew, their old buddy was dead, shot down by a renegade trooper. Only Syrillo knew the truth of the matter, except for the fact that his devious chicanery had gone awry.

Brady was very much alive. Although discretion and the desire to put the past behind him meant that his simmering lust for revenge had been pushed on to the backburner.

The first thing the gang boss knew that his old sidekick was still alive and had been released from custody was gleaned from a newspaper article. He was sitting at a table in the cabin in Gabbs Hole cleaning his revolver when Windy Macaw arrived back from a trip to Virginia City. An easy-going ex-trapper hailing from Utah's Green River country, Macaw bustled in and threw a news sheet down in front of the boss.

He had ridden non-stop after learning of the astonishing news. It was a lurid headline fronting an old copy of the *Virginia Epitaph* that had caught his eye while awaiting his turn in a barber's shop.

'BLACKJACK RELEASED' was more than enough to grab Macaw's attention. After quickly scanning the contents of the article, all thoughts of the bath and haircut were forgotten. Commandeering the paper, he dashed outside, much to the astonishment of the barber and his other customers.

'Brady ain't dead like we all figured,' he gasped out, grabbing a bottle of Moonshine's hooch and tipping a hefty slug down his gullet. 'And not only that. He's served five years and was released from the pen a couple of months back.'

Startled expressions and mutters of surprise greeted the unexpected disclosure. Nobody was more shocked than Kid Syrillo. Culpepper's eyes bulged as he read through the details of the old report. His initial thought was pleasure that one of his best men was still alive. But then another more sinister musing roughly wiped the smile from his face.

His concern was expressed in a brittle growl. 'If'n Brady was released two months ago, why has he not showed up yet?'

The other Blackjacks shifted uncomfortably.

Elko Boon voiced his opinion. 'He could have formed his own gang.'

But Culpepper was having none of that. He shook his head irritably. 'If'n that were the case, we'd have heard about the jobs they've pulled by now. It's some'n else.' His brow creased in thought.

It was left to Moonshine to intone the most worrying aspect of the new revelation. Brady and he had been close. But when the firewater distiller's freedom was at stake, that association counted for nothing.

'The guy could find his way here blindfolded. What's to stop him shopping us to the law and claiming the bounty on our heads.'

That submission produced a grim expression on Culpepper's earthy visage. His eyes narrowed in thought.

'What we gonna do, boss?' whined Chinstrap.

'Shut up and let me think,' rapped the gang leader grabbing the bottle from Macaw's shaking hand. It was another five minutes before he broke the tense silence that had settled over the worried conclave of outlaws. 'What you say makes the most sense, Moonshine,' he said in a measured cadence. 'Looks like our days in Gabbs Hole are numbered. So, we pull one last job then get out of Nevada. We can set up some place else before the law and that double-crossing skunk Brady can catch up with us.'

It was pure coincidence that Culpepper had chosen the bank at Winnemucca as his Nevada swan song.

SIX

SPY ON THE ROOF

The bank manager broke into Cheyenne's anxious musing. 'You seem a little distracted, Mr Brady,' he posited. 'Is something not to your liking in what I have proposed?'

There certainly was something not to his liking. But it had nothing to do with his current dealings with the bank. Rather it was the fact that the bank's financial holdings were being placed in serious jeopardy. And his own hard-earned dough was topping his list of priorities.

He quickly shrugged off the banker's concerns. 'Just thinking about what you said is all.'

What Cheyenne did not cotton to was the fact that Quinn had also spotted him. The outlaw knew that he had been eyeballed. The shock on Brady's face had given him away. Quinn's face remained impassive. No point in letting Brady know. Lucky for him the guy was unarmed. For a fleeting interlude there was a tense stand-off. Neither man had given a hint of anything being amiss.

Quinn was the first to move. He completed his brief enquiry and casually left the premises. The last thing he needed was to be apprehended now.

Once Cheyenne had sussed out the reason for Mesa Quinn's appearance in Winnemucca, he knew what had to be done. Ushering the bemused bank manager back into his office, he rapidly and succinctly appraised him of his suspicions.

Dunstan was nonplussed. This was the first time he had been involved in a potential robbery. And he did not want to be hoodwinked into any hasty decisions. Especially since the information was being furnished by an ex-member of the Blackjacks.

'Are you certain that the man you saw was an outlaw member of your gang?' Dunstan pressed with evident scepticism.

'I am not a member of the gang, Mr Dunstan!' Cheyenne insisted firmly. 'That part of my life is over if'n you recall. It was Mesa Quinn all right. I'd recognize that face anywhere.'

'Then why did you not challenge him there and then?' The bank manager's sibilant accusation was punched out with venom.

'And have him start a gunfight?' Cheyenne replied with a scornful rasp. 'I'm sure you wouldn't want the blood of innocent people on your hands.'

Dunstan realized his error. 'Of course not,' he blustered, quickly changing the subject. 'Well he can't have got far. I'll have the sheriff go after him.'

'Too late for that now,' Cheyenne retorted. 'If'n I know

Quinn, he'll have disappeared as soon as he noticed me.'

More questions followed, much to Brady's irritation. The banker was suspicious and hard to win over. Eventually, after much reasoned persuasion, he allowed himself to be convinced that the blacksmith was sincere. That was when his executive shrewdness took control.

'You wait here,' he said, stepping over to the door and calling the assistant manger into his office from the front counter. Josiah Dunstan was taking no unnecessary risks. 'I will go across and inform the sheriff of what you have said. It is better that this revelation comes from me under the circumstances. I'm sure you will agree with that?'

He did not wait for the other man to reply. Hurrying outside, he quickly crossed the street to the sheriff's office. Various bystanders stopped, curious as to why the portly bank manager was in such an all-fired hurry.

Initially Mesa Quinn's instinct was to split the breeze. Instead, he slipped down the alley beside the bank where he hung around to determine whether his suspicions had substance. He did not have long to wait.

A hawkish eye followed Dunstan's shuffling progress. Quinn scowled as the banker entered the sheriff's office. So he had been right: Brady had seen him and must have spilled the beans. The fat dude was the one who had been attending to Brady. And, judging by his lofty attitude, he had to be the manager. The critters had wasted no time in alerting the law to the potential threat.

The outlaw was nervous. Once again he was sorely tempted to quit the scene before he was discovered. But Mesa Quinn was no milksop. And he was astute enough to know that Culpepper would want him to discover what the law intended doing to prevent the robbery.

Although Brady knew how to reach the gang's hideout in Gabbs Hole, he was also well aware of the precautions exercised to prevent any such assault on the secret domain. A regular system of guards was posted to give warning of any attempted assault or infiltration. After due consideration, Quinn concluded that all the indications pointed to a surprise reception committee being arranged for when the gang made their hit.

The outlaw kept watch for a further half-hour.

Numerous comings and goings occurred between the bank and the other establishments. Panic had laid its icy hold upon the leading citizens of Winnemucca. The dominant figure of Gabe Pershing was the only one to display a cool stance. Quinn could see that the lawman would be the prime instigator of any action taken to thwart the robbery. The sheriff's doughty reputation was well known. If he and Brady got their heads together, the gang would need all their wits to pull this one off successfully.

The outlaw was growing increasingly nervous. He jumped when a dog barked further down the alley. Lingering this close to the bank for much longer was sure to end badly. Being a stranger in Winnemucca, he would soon be noticed and questions would be asked. He needed to find a more secure location from which to observe the action.

Across the street from the bank was a building that appeared to be empty. Displaying a nonchalant mien he assuredly didn't feel, Quinn wandered across making sure that he was unobserved. Wary peepers flicked back and forth. The last thing he needed was for Brady to emerge from the bank and eyeball him. He reached the other side of the street safely.

Ambling down the passageway beside the structure he peered through the dirty windows. There was nobody inside. So he circled around to the rear. A quick look about to ensure he was not being watched, then he slipped through the unlocked door. It took but a moment to mount the stairs and climb out on to the upper veranda. A handy fixed ladder gave access to a flat roof. Luckily, the building also had a false frontage behind which he could hide while observing the street below from his vantage point.

With care, he knew that there was little chance of his being seen. People rarely looked up. Invariably their attention was focused ahead or down. Removing his hat he settled down to observe the proceedings.

Following his disclosure to the the bank manager, Cheyenne had been interviewed by the sheriff. His assurances that the Blackjacks must be intending to launch an imminent raid on the bank had been taken seriously. He left the bank soon after and headed back to the smithy.

Unaware that she was being watched, Jody stood up and joined Brady. An affectionate arm linked in with his as they strolled back up the street together.

A sneer of disdain issued from between Quinn's gritted teeth. He quickly cottoned to the fact that the guy was betraying his old *compadres*. Not only had the treacherous rat shopped them, he had also gotten himself a dame. All very nice and cosy.

The hidden outlaw acknowledged the grim tidings with a sour twist of the lip. If looks could kill the withering grimace would have stabbed the Judas in the back. Instead, the spy's trigger finger tightened on the Winchester clutched in his hands.

One shot and the traitor would be removed. But so would Mesa Quinn. Trapped on the roof of this derelict heap of timber, his number would also be called. Better to sit it out and see what happened.

Meanwhile, the leading lights of the Winnemucca town council had gathered at the bank. They were seated around a large table in the conference room above. Anxious looks passed between the council members. This sort of thing was outside their remit. They were businessmen. All eyes swung towards the imposing figure of the sheriff who stood up to address the meeting.

Before he had the chance to open his mouth, a staccato voice snapped. 'So what are you going to do about it, Sheriff?' It was Amos Wendover who voiced what each man was thinking. The mayor's anxiety was palpable as he mopped the sweat from his face. 'Our livelihoods are at stake here. This bank holds all our savings.' Mutters of accord greeted this obvious statement.

Pershing coughed. His dour features assumed a granite-like toughness. Here was his opportunity to secure a reputation beyond the borders of Nevada. Pull it off and his name would be headline news. It might even come to rival that of his hero Wyatt Earp. Pershing couldn't resist a wry smile at the thought.

The bank manager noticed the half-concealed smirk and took it the wrong way.

'This is not a laughing matter, Sheriff,' rapped Dunstan. 'If you need extra help, we can always call in the army to help secure our safety.'

'That will not be necessary,' replied the lawman, quickly composing his expression into a suitable aspect of sobriety. 'I can handle this perfectly well, with your assistance of course.'

'So what have you in mind?' interjected Wendover impatiently. 'That brigand could be massing with his cronies nearby even as we speak.'

Having consulted with Brady, Sheriff Pershing had decided to kill two birds with one stone. Pull this off and he would be assured of victory at the next election together with a hefty pay rise. His plan of action had come from the mouth of the ex-Blackjack. Now he could take full credit for the scheme.

Pershing had been sceptical at first thinking that Brady might be bluffing. Sure, the guy had reported the unexpected appearance of his old associate. Although that could be a ploy enabling him to pass on any planned operation to capture the gang. If that were the case, why bother to say anything about a gang member being spotted? There was no need for that.

The more he thought about it, the more Pershing became convinced that the new blacksmith had indeed turned over a new leaf. The sheriff had also been won over by the man's charismatic pull.

And he was not the only one to be charmed by the newcomer.

Everybody in town was aware of the magnetic attraction that had developed between Brady and Jody Dunstan. Only two people had exhibited deep reservations concerning the liaison.

Her father's distrust of the ex-Blackjack was under-standable. And most folks knew that Mayor Wendover harboured designs on the girl. Pershing knew that any plan put forward by the reformed outlaw would receive short shrift from the town's leading citizen.

Brady's plan, however, certainly had merit, so the sheriff was prepared to exert all his influence on the assembly to bring it to fruition as his own idea.

Another cough as he gathered his thoughts. Then he launched into what he had in mind.

'My suggestion is that we transfer all the bank's funds over to the jailhouse and lock it in one of the cells. A couple of guards can be left to watched over it. In the meantime, myself and a posse will remain in the bank ready to ambush the gang when they arrive.'

He looked around to gauge the reaction to his scheme.

Muttering broke out as members of the council debated the issue amongst themselves.

Pershing allowed them a few minutes before butting in. 'Well, gentlemen, does my suggestion merit your approval?'

'Sure sounds good to me,' concurred a dapper little man called Cabel Sankey who ran the Birdcage Hotel.

'Just so long as you have plenty of men who can handle a gun ready to give these varmints a hot reception,' added Dench, the storekeeper.

'I'm sure there are enough men in Winnemucca who are able and willing to protect the town's interests,' replied the sheriff. He then addressed his next proposi-tion to Amos Wendover. 'It would considerably help our situation, Mr Mayor, if'n you were to offer a fee to those men willing to place themselves in danger.'

Wendover huffed some. But the rest of council over-ruled any adverse comments. And it was left to the Reverend Micah Fanshaw to summarize their thoughts in a deeply sonorous baritone. 'If men are prepared to place their lives on the line in order to help save our assets, the least the town can do is to express its gratitude by paying a satisfactory remuneration.'

Pershing rubbed his hands. 'It's settled then?' Nods all round, including one from a somewhat abashed Amos Wendover. 'Then we need to set things in motion without any further delay.'

'I will need to make a record of all the money bags as they are filled and transferred,' Dunstan declared firmly. Beady eyes peered over the top of his steel-rimmed spectacles. This was an unprecedented event that would require all his financial expertise to carry through. Like the sheriff, success could lead to recognition and in his case the managership of a much larger branch, perhaps in Virginia City.

'And I will need an escort of trustworthy men to effect that transfer. This is a most unusual occurrence and head office will demand a full report. Therefore everything must be conducted with security in mind.'

'Best that you set things in motion without delay, Josiah,' said the sheriff rising to his feet. 'Let me know as soon as you are ready to move.'

Chairs scraped back as the meeting followed his example and broke up. Soon after, the line of councillors filed out of the bank heading off to their own establishments.

On the roof of the derelict building, Mesa Quinn stirred himself. Things below were starting to hot up. It was another half hour before a group of six well-armed men filed into the bank. They each wore the badge of a deputy town marshal. Soon after they emerged in pairs. Each twosome carried between them a leather bag embossed with the well-known gold leaf emblem of the Nevada Central Reserve.

Those bags looked mighty heavy. Quinn's eyes bulged. A silky tongue slid across his upper lip evincing avaricious thirst for all that lovely dough. He followed its progress across the street to the jail. The other posse members followed in quick succession.

So that was their plan: hide the money in the jail and wait for the outlaws to enter the bank where a lethal reception committee would be waiting. Such a scheme must have been thought up by that treacherous half-breed. All that Mesa Quinn needed to find out now was how many men were guarding the money in the jail.

As he made to leave his elevated hideout, a further six men arrived at the bank armed with rifles and shotguns. They were taking no chances of losing their quarry. Quinn's lean features broke into a broad grin. They were going to have a long wait.

Sidling out the back door of the derelict building, the outlaw picked a delicate course through the array of back lots and shacks behind the main street. He did not meet a soul apart from a tethered mule that merely watched him with bored apathy as he passed.

On reaching the back of the jail, special care was needed to avoid detection. He was about to approach the gated backyard when a visitor sauntered round the corner to his left. Just in the nick of time, Quinn ducked down behind a row of barrels.

The visitor went across the yard and knocked on the cellblock door with the butt of his pistol. It was answered by a tall rangy dude sporting a luxuriant handlebar moustache. But more importantly, he was holding a sawn-off shotgun. Quinn listened intently to the conversation.

'What can I do for you, Shorty?' asked the guard.

'Gabe sent me over to see if'n you fellas need any extra help in here,' the newcomer informed the jailhouse guard. 'We have a dozen men already in the bank and are taking it in shifts to keep a continuous watch until these robbers show up.'

Nyle Forrest shook his head. 'Me and Rowdy Bill oughta be enough. It's you guys at the bank that's gonna see all the action.'

'Where you storing the money?' asked Shorty Plummer.

Forrest slung a thumb behind him. 'We're keeping it locked up in the rear cell.' He squared his shoulders slapping a hand on the butt of his weapon. 'Anybody tries muscling in here and they'll get a load of buckshot up their ass.'

At that moment the other guard known as Rowdy Bill called out from the front office. 'Who's that you're talking to, Nyle?'

'Only Shorty Plummer who's come over from the bank. Wants to know if'n we need any more help in here.'

Bill grunted. 'Thought so. All that guy wants is an easy life.' Then he retired back to reading his newspaper and nursing a bottle of whiskey.

'Let's hope this goes on for a few days,' replied Plummer. 'The daily fee they're paying us is more than I earn in a week of grafting for that skinflint Norbert Dench.'

'Just so long as you capture the bastards,' muttered Forrest. 'I have all my savings tied up with the bank.'

'Or kill them,' Plummer interjected firmly. 'I hear tell most of them varmints have a price on their heads. And we'll cop a share of that.'

'Never thought of that,' grinned Forrest. 'Reckon I'll take a look through the sheriff's stack of wanted dodgers and work out what's coming to us.'

A few more remarks of a general nature followed. Then Shorty Plummer bade his colleague a hearty farewell.

SEVEN

JAILHOUSE ROCK

Quinn rubbed his hands.

That couldn't have gone better if'n he had planned it himself. The unsuspecting guards had revealed a heap of vital information. Not only that, now he had names which would make securing access to the jailhouse all the easier.

He slipped away making a tortuous detour to avoid any undesirable encounters. A keen memory helped him to picture the route in reverse for when the robbery took place.

It was a long ride back to Gabbs Hole. Quinn rode all through the first night, dozing in the saddle until sheer exhaustion forced him to rest up in the shade of some cottonwoods. When he arrived back at the hideout, the boss was eager to hear his news. Quinn was given little time to recover. A belt of Moonshine's potent brew, however, soon revived him.

Under the urgent barrage of questions from

Culpepper, the spy revealed all that he had seen and heard.

'You certain the money is being stashed in the jail?' Culpepper was quite stunned at the revelations brought back by his highly esteemed confederate. He had expected to pull off a regular bank robbery. What Quinn had revealed changed all that. 'It sure would be a smart break if'n we were to lift the dough from right under their noses.' Greedy flecks glinted in the gang leader's eyes.

His large snout twitched with anticipation of a big haul. Just as important to Rafe Culpepper, however, was the surefire expectation of widespread publicity that would result due to the audacious nature of the heist. The Blackjacks would then be talked of in the same hushed tones as the notorious Missouri gang led by Jesse James.

'That's the durned truth, boss,' insisted Quinn. 'And I'm also certain that Brady spotted me. It was a shock seeing him talking with the bank manager cool as you please.'

'So why didn't he call you out?' snapped Jackknife Stringer.

Quinn scoffed at the cynical remark. 'He wasn't armed. And you know what the critter was like: he used to think of himself as a new Robin Hood.'

Numerous baffled expressions greeted this piece of history. The ex-bank teller sighed. 'You guys ought to read more than just dime novels. He's an English guy who robbed the rich and gave to the poor.'

'That sure has got to be us, boys,' interjected Culpepper grinning widely. The remark elicited a hearty round of laughter.

Quinn joined in with the ribald hurrawing before completing his description. 'It also means that Brady didn't want any shooting of innocent bystanders. That was another thing Robin Hood was famous for. The Kid found that out to his cost.'

Syrillo blushed. He hated being reminded of his ignominious loss of face. But what haunted the Kid most was the fact that Cheyenne Brady was still alive, and, as long as that was the case, he couldn't rest easy. At some point during the coming assault on the Winnemucca bank he would have to find a way to settle things with Brady once and for all.

Nevertheless, the Kid's hackles were up. He was more than ready for a fight.

'Seems to me you have that snout of your'n stuck in a book too much for your own good, pen-pusher,' he snarled, jumping to his feet. 'Real men let their guns do the talking.'

'And look where it got you,' rasped Quinn who, though a man of letters, was well capable of holding his own in any fracas.

The broadcloth suit might have been a tad trail-weary but it fitted him well. His ability to blend into all shades of society had been a vital asset when investigating potential bank targets in the past. On the remote frontier of the American West the wearing of a gunbelt did not arouse any suspicions: it was an accepted part of a man's attire. Many respectable businessmen wore them for show.

Not so Mesa Quinn who was always ready to use his irons when the need arose.

He pushed back his own chair now, prepared to meet

the Kid face to face.

'That was one reckless action,' he snarled, fastening a derisory glare on to the younger man. 'Gunning down the dame could have done for the rest of us. It's lucky we have the Hole to hide out in. Posses were searching high and low for the Blackjacks after that.'

Rafe Culpepper stepped between them.

'Save your quarrel for later. This job is more important than any petty squabbling.' The gang leader didn't need to raise his voice nor draw his pistol. 'Until then, we all work together.' A stony expression drilled into both protagonists forcing them to back down.

'Just tell this jerk to keep his comments about me under wraps,' grumbled Syrillo.

'You heard the guy,' Culpepper concurred quickly, pulling everyone's thoughts back to the matter in hand. 'Now what else do we need to know?'

Quinn knew better than to argue. But a brisk glare aimed in the Kid's direction signified that he was ready to continue the argument at any time.

Then he carried on relating his amazing news. 'Brady seems to have established himself as an honest citizen. He don't want to rock the boat. That's the reason he didn't blow my cover as a prospective customer. And, seeing as I was the only one present wearing a gunbelt, the lead was sure to fly if'n he had.' Another wry grimace headed Kid Syrillo's way.

Quinn then went on to relay the unusual occurrences that eventually found him overhearing the jailhouse guards unwittingly divulging their plans for the bank's money. The rest of the gang sat open-mouthed as they listened to the bizarre revelations.

After he had finished, Culpepper accepted the explanation with a brisk nod.

'You done well, Mesa,' he praised the ex-bank teller. 'Now that we know the stunt they're hoping to pull, we can outfox them with one of our own tricks.'

'What you got in mind, boss?' asked Windy Macaw who was oiling his revolver.

'If what Mesa has said is correct, we need to get into the jail through the back door.' His brow furrowed in thought mulling over the implications. 'All the attention will be focused on the bank which they will be expecting us to hit.'

It was Moonshine who posed the obvious problem. 'The jail door will be locked. We need to find some way to make the guard open up. Trying to blast our way in will raise too much of a ruckus. Those guys waiting inside the bank will suss what's happening and come a-running with all guns blazing.'

For the next half-hour, it was discussed at length. Schemes, both practical and fanciful, were tossed around. Culpepper was always a willing listener to what his men had to suggest. From the array of ideas, a coherent strategy was finally worked out.

'We'll head out at first light,' he decided, once the scheme had been settled. 'It'll take three days to reach Winnemucca. We want to hit them at first light. They'll all be tired out not knowing when we're going to pay them a visit.' He chuckled to himself. 'I'd love to see Brady's face when he finds out the Blackjacks have scuppered his plans to catch us out.'

'It'll be the town dignitaries who are hopping mad

when they discover we've lifted the dough from right under their whiskey-bloated noses,' added Elko Boon.

The comment elicited more hearty guffaws. Culpepper joined in. He sniffed, giving his own prominent appendage a playful rub.

'Better get some sleep, boys,' he said with a yawn. 'We've gotten a busy few days ahead of us. Then we can all take a long vacation.'

'Amen to that,' snorted Chinstrap.

The new day dawned fine and clear.

Big-Nose Rafe drew on a quirly as he surveyed the slumbering town of Winnemucca below. Streaks of purple, pink and orange announced the imminent arrival of the main participant. As if on cue, the sun poked its head above the serated rim of the Jackapoo Mountains. Bloody Run Peak stood out proud and statuesque against the backdrop of iridescent colouring. A mind-boggling tableau for those of an artistic bent.

But the gang were after more tangible rewards.

They had made camp the previous night within a copse of trees overlooking the town on a low hillock. It had been a cold supper for them all. Culpepper was taking no chances of the flickering light cast by a fire giving away their presence.

Nothing moved down below. The town appeared deserted. An illusion as they all knew. Guards would be waiting inside the bank ready for the expected raid. Culpepper chuckled to himself. They were going to be sadly disappointed.

Mesa Quinn pointed out the direction they needed to

take for the approach to the jailhouse.

'Going in from this angle, the guards inside the bank won't be able to spot us.'

'Let's ride then, boys,' the boss directed, strolling across to the picket line. 'Time to make a name for ourselves. Not to mention a hefty wedge of dough.'

In single file, the line of riders made its way down to the edge of the built-up area where Culpepper ordered them to dismount. 'You take the lead,' Quinn was told. 'Can you recall the way through this mess of back lots?'

The ex-bank teller tapped his head. 'Perfect memory inside here, boss. I know ever twist and turn better than my own mother.'

'Didn't know you had one,' remarked the Kid acidly, enjoying the numerous sniggers engendered by the riposte.

'Cut out the smart stuff!' growled Culpepper, effectively stifling the hilarity. 'From here on, the only comments I want are about the job. And keep them down to brief whispers. Anybody blows this caper and they're dead meat.' His flinty gaze swept over the assembled outlaws. 'Now let's move.'

Quinn was true to his word. It was now light enough to avoid any of the myriad obstacles scattered across their path.

Snaking through the chaotic amalgam of hutments, corrals and rubbish tips, he led them unerringly to the rear of the jail. No human interference was encountered to hinder their progress. Only a couple of mouse-hunting cats and a wary mongrel paid them any heed.

The jail was easy to spot with its high wall surrounding

the prison exercise yard. The solid door was shut fast. There was no lock which meant that it was bolted from the inside. Being the smallest and most lithe member of the gang, Elko Boon was the obvious choice to climb over the wall.

Moving his horse up beside the wall, Boon stood up on the saddle and hauled himself on to the flat top. A line of curious black crows watched with interest. Luckily there was no line of broken glass to make the task more dangerous. He slipped down to the far side and soon had the door open.

Culpepper quickly gave further orders. 'Moonshine and Chinstrap.' The two outlaws stepped forward. 'You two go round to the front and keep an eye on the bank. If'n anybody comes out and heads this way, one of you come a-running fast. Leave your horses here. The Kid can look after them while the rest of us go grab the dough.'

The two men nodded, handing the reins of their mounts to the surly young hothead. They then slunk away round the side of the jail towards the main street.

Syrillo snorted. A flick of his dirty blond hair indicated his displeasure at being given what he considered to be a menial job.

Culpepper's back stiffened. His teeth ground with malice. This was no time for the Kid's puerile antics.

'Listen up, knucklehead!' A rough hand grabbed the Kid's shirt front causing a button to pop. Pushing his large snout to within an inch of the sneering tearaway, he snarled,'I ain't got time for no childish tantrums. Do as you're damn well told or Jackknife here gets to practise his throwing skills. Got my drift?'

Stringer flicked the knife into the air and caught it with the other hand. A rancid smile split the angular contours of his emaciated features. The threat of an imminent and deathly silent encounter with the bladerunner's favoured weapon instantly secured the Kid's attention, wiping the scowl from his face.

'I didn't mean nothing, Rafe,' he blustered lifting his shoulders. 'Just hoped to be in on the action is all.'

'Whatever job is doled out by me is important for this caper to succeed,' he growled out, struggling to keep his anger in check. The gravelly tones were biting, edged with an abrasive cut. 'And this sure ain't the place to start any ructions.'

He didn't bother to register the Kid's reaction to the terse reprimand. Any disciplinary action could wait until the job was completed. Instead he croaked out in a harsh undertone, 'You others come with me.'

Guns drawn, the five outlaws stole across the yard to the back door giving access to the cell block. On the far side of the yard stood a gallows, its macabre presence issuing a silent yet menacing caveat to those who strayed outside the law. Boon shivered forcing himself to look away. This was no time for wavering scruples to niggle at his choice of lifestyle.

They had discussed the tactic to be adopted before leaving Gabbs Hole.

Sucking in a deep lungful of air, Culpepper rapped sharply on the door with the butt of his revolver. He heard the scraping of a chair from inside. Seconds later a muted voice called from inside, 'Who's there?'

'It's me, Shorty Plummer,' hissed the gang leader

80

aiming a sly wink at Mesa Quinn who had informed him of the guard's nasal twang. He deliberately coughed to conceal his own guttural tones. 'Is that you, Nyle?' He didn't wait for an answer. 'The sheriff has gotten more men than he needs over there at the moment. So he's told me to spell you guys. Give you a chance to go home and get some'n to eat. One at a time, of course.'

The thick door effectively blurred his voice.

'Sounds good to me, Shorty,' came back the breezy reply. 'You sound a mite hoarse.'

'Just a sore throat is all,' croaked Culpepper, grinning at his associates.

'We could sure do with a change of scene for a couple of hours,' added Forrest as he stuck a key in the door lock.

Rafe and the other Blackjacks tensed, their guns cocked and at the ready.

As soon as the door opened they pushed inside. Macaw struck the startled guard over the head with his gun barrel laying him out cold. Quinn then searched his clothing for the all-important keys to the cell where the bags of money were stashed.

'Hurry it up, Mesa,' hissed Culpepper. 'We ain't got all day.'

'They're not on him,' announced Quinn.

'Let me see,' growled Culpepper pushing him aside. But he had no luck either. 'Damn it!' he cursed. 'They must be with the other guy in the front office.'

'Call for him to come through,' the gang boss hissed. 'Say you're the bank cashier.'

The directive was aimed at Quinn who had the most cultured voice of the outlaws. It had been perfected during his time dealing with high profile customers when serving as a legitmate bank employee. It was a factor that had led to much joshing before the gang realized he was a vital asset to their continued success.

'I'll grab him as soon as he appears,' Culpepper said, moving behind the door leading into the office. 'You boys prop up this dude to look as if he's leaning against the wall.'

Quinn tried to put on a sophisticated accent that was meant to emulate a banker.

But unlike Forrest, Rowdy Bill was no dull-witted lackey as his nickname might have implied. He instantly recognized the phoney inflection. Quinn had made the error of trying over hard to impress. The guard had rightly concluded that somehow the Blackjacks must have discovered the money was being stored in the jail. He cursed. It had to be that double-dealing blacksmith.

Bill drew his pistol. He sucked in a deep breath backing nervously towards the outer door. Once out on the main street, he gave vent to his fears hollering out in the raucus timbre that was well known in the locality.

'Sheriff, Sheriff, shift your ass and come quick! Those jaspers have broken into the jailhouse.' Frantically waving his arms like a crazy roadrunner, Rowdy Bill hurried down the middle of street towards the bank.

EIGHT

VENGEANCE TRAIL

Chinstrap, who was keeping an eye on the bank with his buddy, panicked at sight of this demented fiend running down the street. A brace of shots was loosed at the ranting guard who took one in the shoulder. He spun round and collapsed on the ground.

But any chance of thwarting Rowdy Bill's alarm had come too late.

The ruckus had been heard by the guards waiting inside the bank. They were not slow to respond as rifles were poked through the windows. The early morning silence was shattered by the thunder of guns as a lethal barrage poured forth. Chinstrap had made the mistake of stepping out from behind the gate where he was concealed. That exposure cost him his life. He was chopped down by half-a-dozen .44.40 bullets.

Keeping his head down, old Moonshine peered out from cover. He emptied his revolver at the bank before retreating back down the alley reloading his pistol on the move. It was a deft operation that was not easy to master. Yet any gunslinger worth his salt needed to perfect the practice to survive the hazardous life he had chosen.

Inside the jail, Culpepper knew that his plans for a stealthy and uncomplicated heist had been dashed. There was no need for secrecy any longer.

'Stand back!' he rapped, pointing his gun at the cell-door lock. Two sharp blasts and the mechanism was blown asunder. 'Get those bags and let's scarper. Jackknife, you keep a watch out for any of those bank guards coming in through the front.'

Quinn, Macaw and Elko Boon snatched up one of the heavy bags apiece while Culpepper ran outside and called for Kid Syrillo to bring the horses inside the yard. But there was no response to his summons.

'What you doing out there, Kid?' he shouted. 'Get those nags in here and help us load up the dough. Those varmints will be sniffing round our tails any second.'

Still no response.

That was when Moonshine appeared in the doorway on the far side of the yard.

'Where's that blasted Kid?' rasped Culpepper, his normal level-headed guise rapidly disintegrating along with his plans.

Moonshine had been hot-footing it back to the jail when he spotted the Kid mounting up and riding off in the opposite direction. The old reprobate realized that the young tearaway had panicked when the gunfire shattered the dream of an easy heist. Moonshine growled out a rabid curse dispatching a shell at the lily-livered absconder. It buzzed past the Kid's head, but failed to halt his flight.

The other horses milled about in confusion threatening to stampede.

Moonshine managed to gathered up their reins before any damage was done. Poking his head round the doorpost into the prison yard, he called out. 'That darned Kid has run out on us, boss. But I've managed to corral the horses.'

'Bring them over here,' Culpepper ordered, 'These bags are durned heavy.'

More shooting broke out inside the jailhouse. The gruff voice of Sheriff Pershing cut through the harsh rattle of gunfire. 'You can't get away. Surrender now if'n you want to save your hides. We have you surrounded. Try to resist and we'll wipe you out like the verminous scum you are.'

Stringer backed out of the cellblock working his six-shooter. He had the satisfaction of hearing a scream of pain. The hit was sufficient to delay any further attack from that direction. But it could only be a temporary reprieve. The writing was on the wall.

Rafe Culpepper knew that the game was up. He emptied his own revolver at the deputies milling round the cellblock exit driving them back inside.

With the cat well and truly out of the bag, there was no time left for them to load up the money bags. Stay here and they were dog meat. He cursed his impotence loudly for having to abandon the heist. But there was no alternative if they were to escape unscathed.

'Mount up, boys,' he shouted. 'It's every man for himself. We'll meet back at the hideout.'

Swinging up on to their saddles, the remaining gang

members spurred towards the narrow rear exit from the prison yard. Last man out was old Moonshine. Age had slowed him down. And by the time his turn came to leave, the sheriff and his men had emerged from the cellblock.

'Get the bastards,' bellowed the lawman. His men did not need any encouragement to let fly with all their weapons.

Bullets zipped and winged around the old brigand. But it was not to be his lucky day. Moonshine did not stand a chance under such a storm of hot lead. His back was peppered with holes, blood erupting from a myriad fatal strikes.

Ignoring the downed outlaw, the guards, led by the angry sheriff hurried across the yard. Outside, they were just in time to see the last outlaw disappearing behind a shed. A futile volley of shots were dispatched, more out of frustration than any hope of scoring a hit.

Meanwhile, heading in the opposite direction, Kid Syrillo had materialized on to the main street. To his good fortune, he was a half-dozen blocks further west of where all the action was taking place. So nobody noticed him. Swinging left, he gave his mount a vicious dig and sent it scurrying off towards the opposite end of Winnemucca.

However, the braggart's cowardly abandonment of his buddies had not gone unnoticed.

Cheyenne Brady had been ordered to remain on the premises of his blacksmith's shop while the planned ambush of the Blackjacks was in progress. No amount of exhortations that he was a changed man had cut any ice with the suspicious dignitaries of the town council. It mattered not that he was the one who had blown the whistle on the gang's most likely intentions.

It was all down to Amos Wendover. The toad had insisted that he be held under virtual house arrest. Not that Cheyenne particularly minded. He was still able to continue his work assisted by the eager Sourdough Lamar.

And frequent visits by Jody had considerably helped pass the time. Even though her father had tried to thwart their meetings, Jody had studiously disregarded his order. The room above the smithy had become a rendezvous for numerous romantic trysts.

Cheyenne was thinking of their next amorous tête-à-tête at which he intended to raise their relationship to a new level over supper and a glass of wine. His dreamy musings were violently interrupted by the unmistakable clatter of gunfire. And it was clearly coming from outside the bank. He rushed across to the window and peered out.

Unfortunately, from this angle he was unable to see what was happening. Frustration at being confined to his quarters threatened to boil over. He slammed a bunched fist against the wall. Seconds later a horse and rider emerged from a nearby alley.

Cheyenne's musing was given a jolt when he recognized the hunched figure of Kid Syrillo. It was over five years since he had last set eyes on the gutless whelp who had gunned him down. The Kid was older and more careworn, but there was no mistaking those sly features.

Syrillo dragged his horse to a skittering halt outside the smithy. Turning round, he looked back towards the bank. The grimace of terror written across his youthful features was writ large. So was his reason for being out front and removed from any immediate danger. The craven rat had deserted his buddies in their hour of need.

Cheyenne immediately drew the conclusion that the robbery was not going in the gang's favour. And Syrillo had abandoned ship.

Confirming his interpretation of the Kid's motives, the Judas spurred off down the street heading west. A feeling of anger and resentment bubbled up inside the ex-Blackjack's chest. There out front was the reason for all his anguish in recent years. And, once again, the lowlife tearaway was escaping justice.

Well this time he was going to pay dearly for his cowardice.

Strapping on the gunbelt that had lain idle for so long, Cheyenne dashed downstairs where old Sourdough was stoking up the furnace. The rattle of gunfire had not phased the old timer one jot. He was enjoying his freedom. No way was he going back to a life on the prod. In any case, he was getting too old for being chased by posses.

'What's bugging you, boy?' the old timer called out, while vigorously pumping the bellows. 'Looks like you've done seen a ghost.'

'That sure weren't no spectre that just rode off up the street,' Cheyenne replied while quickly saddling his horse. 'Didn't you see him?'

'Who?'

'Kid Syrillo, the waster who shot me down leaving me for dead. He's just abandoned the gang. It looks like the heist has gone wrong and he's turned chicken and quit.' Brady hawked a lump of spit on to the ground. 'Well, I'm going after him.'

'You watch yourself,' advised the brooding blacksmith. 'That Kid is a no-good coyote from what you've told me, slippery and devious like a desert fox.'

Cheyenne nodded then rode out of the front door of the smithy and swung left in the direction taken by his quarry.

He was not alone. The Kid's sudden appearance on the main street must have been spotted by some of those guarding the bank. A group of men came running down towards the smithy.

'Hey, that's Brady, ain't it?' shouted Wendover.

'Sure looks like him,' answered Norbert Dench.

'And it looks like he's escaping with that other bandit,' added Sankey, the hotelier.

'Stop right now,' ordered Sheriff Pershing. 'We've gotten you covered.'

But Cheyenne was too fired up to heed the warnings.

He spurred off after the Kid.

No further warnings were issued as Pershing raised his rifle. Three shots rang out. Cheyenne swung his mount from side to side trying to avoid the bullets. But one struck his horse in the neck.

The animal went down throwing its rider into the dust. Brady staggered to his feet only to be roughly grabbed by a dozen hands. He was quickly disarmed. With little regard for his welfare, he was frog-marched back up the street, the sheriff's gun jabbing in his ribs. Angry fists pummelled his body.

'I'll deal with this,' snapped Pershing pushing the assailants off.

'I knew this varmint was no good,' rasped Wendover,

ignoring the sheriff as he aimed a punch of his own at the tethered captive. It caught Brady on the side of the head stunning him. Others once again quickly joined in with the manhandling.

'Let's string the bastard up,' shouted Cabel Sankey eager to show his displeasure now that any danger was past.

'Keep back I said,' railed Pershing, helping the prisoner to his feet. Brandishing his rifle, he pushed the milling crowd back. 'There'll be no vigilante law while I'm sheriff in this town.'

Brady shook the mush from his head. He needed to get the truth out into the open, and quick before this lynch-happy mob overwhelmed the lone figure of law and order.

'You've got this all wrong,' he stressed. 'I was chasing after one of the outlaws who was escaping. How many times do I have to say it? I'm not with that gang anymore.' But his vehement exhortations of innocence were drowned out. Trying to persuade these turkeys of his innocence was like pissing into the wind.

'A likely story,' huffed Wendover pushing forward. 'You were trying to escape knowing we had foiled the robbers. It's just a pity the other critter managed to escape. But at least we've caught you.'

'But not before poor old Rowdy Bill was gunned down,' snarled Rubin McGill. That earned Cheyenne more abuse.

The sheriff was becoming anxious that the situation was getting out of hand. He had been involved in mob rule while serving as a deputy with Bear River Tom Smith in Abilene, Kansas. A similar situation had quickly threatened to explode when ropes were produced and the

90

hanging of an accused man was imminent. Only through Smith's forceful character was the rabid crowd persuaded that the law should follow its official course.

Gabe Pershing hoped that he would have a similar influence now.

By the time they reached the jail, a large crowd had gathered. Their mood was becoming increasingly charged. Pershing stood on the boardwalk waving his gun.

'Keep back!' he shouted. 'This man will get what's coming to him in a court of law if'n he's found guilty.'

'The circuit judge ain't due for another month,' called out a voice from the back. 'I say we do the job now and be done with it.'

Irate cheers of support rang out through the early morning mist. Dogs barked and mules brayed in the highly fraught atmosphere. The crowd surged forward.

That was when Jody Dunstan pushed her way to the front and stepped up beside the sheriff and his prisoner. 'The sheriff is right,' she exhorted the crowd. 'It is for the law to decide if he is guilty. But I can assure you that this man has done nothing wrong.'

But her pleas for calm and rational decision-making were lost amidst the raucous spleen of the baying throng. All seemed lost. Gabe Pershing was no Bear River Smith. He felt out of his depth.

Then a loud blast cut through the tense setting. It was immediately followed by a harsh whiskey-soured grating. 'Next critter to move gets the second barrel in his guts.'

The stark warning came from behind a wagon on the opposite side of the street behind which Sourdough Lamar was secreted. The crowd turned as one to face this new intrusion. The blunt order had silenced their hostile intimidation. But only temporarily.

A man at the rear of the crowd who was not in the immediate firing line urged the rest to ignore the intruder's defiance.

'He's only one man. He can't gun us all down. So what are we waiting for?'

But those at the front were less eager to challenge the buckshot in Lamar's double-barrelled twelve gauge that could be seen poking out from the side of the wagon. The ex-con backed up his invective with a further warning. 'I got two more guns here. Who's gonna be the first to make their acquaintance?'

In support of his taunt, Lamar loosed off a couple of pistol shots, one of which removed the mayor's stovepipe hat. That was enough for Amos Wendover who was at the front of the crowd. Splaying out his arms, he urged the crowd to pull back.

Lamar took advantage of the brief lull to call his partner over to join him.

Cheyenne did not need a second bidding. Stay here and he was going to be the chief guest at his very own necktie party. He squeezed Jody's arm offering her a grateful smile. But this was no place to linger. His partner had two horses saddled and waiting behind the wagon.

'Mount up and light out,' Lamar urged him, 'while I keep these buzzards at arm's length.'

'I ain't going no place without you, pard,' replied Brady with vigour. 'We go together or stay and fight it out.'

'Then let's ride like the wind before these jiggers

recover their backbones.'

Both men leapt on to their horses and spurred off down the street. A few bullets were dispatched above the heads of the crowd encouraging them to scatter.

The last face Brady saw as he looked back was that of Jody Dunstan. Her pale complexion was drawn and tear-stained. A lone hand was raised in a gesture of farewell. Would they ever again be together? That hope was now in the lap of the gods.

Then she and the rest of the virulent throng were lost in the swirling tendrils of early morning white mist.

The two men rode hard for an hour, pushing their mounts until Cheyenne knew they needed to take a breather. West of Winnemucca the trail rose gradually until it emerged from the mist levelling out on the arid Black Rock plateau. In all directions a sandy wasteland stretched away to the horizon. Cheyenne's intense gaze probed the eastern panorama to determine whether a posse was on their trail.

He was relieved that no movement broke the static terrain.

'This is where we part company,' he declared to his sidekick.

The announcement came as a surprise to Lamar. 'I thought we were partners,' the old prospector muttered in a crestfallen voice.

'And so we are,' Brady assured him. 'But I'm going after Kid Syrillo. There's unfinished business between the two of us that needs sorting.' Lamar knew exactly what that business entailed. 'I'll meet you at Stonewall Flats. That's the nearest town to Gabbs Hole.'

'What in thunder are you going back there for?' exclaimed the startled old prospector. 'Those guys think you welched on them. They'll gun you down for sure.'

'Not when I tell them that I've hunted down the Kid and have seen the error of my ways. And Rafe can't prove that I helped the townsfolk protect their dough. I reckon he'll welcome me back into the gang after hearing that I was nearly lynched.' Brady rolled a stogie and lit up. 'It's bound to be reported in the papers. Us trying to go straight will be viewed as a ruse to suss out the bank for the Blackjacks to rob.'

'So do you think he'll let me join the gang?' Lamar asked gingerly.

'When I tell him how you saved my bacon back there, you'll be the toast of Gabbs Hole.'

'Gee!' he exclaimed, somewhat startled at this new development. 'Do you reckon that joining up with the Nevada Blackjacks will be a feather in my hat?'

Cheyenne slung a leg over his saddle horn and leaned on it.

Drawing on the stogie he contemplated the claims he had just made. A pensive frown brought his thick eyebrows together as he thought about whether Big-Nose Rafe would be so accommodating to his old sidekick.

The gang leader was a capable outlaw. But he was also a loose cannon, a jasper prone to wild spates of temper and outlandish behaviour. The bizarre holding of the boxing match between himself and the Kid was typical of the volatile gang boss. Rather than welcoming him back into the gang, Culpepper might just as easily gun him down in cold blood.

Such thoughts were best kept under wraps for the time being.

'Don't be too keen, Sourdough,' he cautioned wagging a finger. 'Remember that we'll only be there to help bring the gang to justice.'

Lamar's face dropped. But he realized that his partner was right.

'Guess I'm too long on the tooth anyways to be a notorious owlhoot.'

Before going their separate ways, the old timer voiced his concerns regarding his partner's forthcoming showdown.

'How will you know where to find the Kid?' he queried.

'Syrillo hails from Wagonfire up north in the Oregon country where his father is a preacher,' explained Brady. 'My figuring is that he's scared and will head for home.' He shrugged as another thought occurred to him. 'I'll soon find out when I reach the next town.'

'That'll be Jackpot,' declared Sourdough. 'The town got its name when an old buddy of mine happened to spot a gold nugget in King Creek. In less time than it takes to say paydirt, the place was booming. Prospectors flooded in from all over the territory. Me included.'

'Any luck?' enquired Cheyenne with a grin and already knowing the answer.

'Too late as usual,' sighed the old-timer. 'All the best claims had been grabbed.'

Cheyenne nodded. But he was more concerned with the coming showdown.

'Those straggling blond locks of his and the curling moustache are a dead giveaway. Somebody is bound to have spotted him. If not, then I'll have to keep looking.'

'*Adios* then, pard.' Lamar tipped his hat as the younger man rode off into the desert. The old-timer watched until he disappeared behind a soaring butte. Then he swung his own mount to the south. It was a three day ride to reach Stonewall Flats. He idly speculated how long he would need to hang around before Brady joined him.

NINE

REFLECTION
OF LUCK

Jackpot lay on the far side of the Black Rock desert.

The town had long since ceased to be the boom town it was when Sourdough Lamar took up residence there. The gold had dried up and the miners had moved on. Only those who had managed to secure a more permanent source of income remained, mainly through the less alluring exploitation of the pine clad slopes that soared up on either side of King Creek. Sawmills now processed the wood and shipped it out by wagon.

Inevitably, all the buildings were constructed from timber. Numerous rotting skeletons of abandoned huts littered the banks of the creek, a testament to the short term mining boom. Cheyenne noticed that one or two were still occupied, their inhabitants still clinging to the illusory dream of hitting paydirt.

He nudged his horse down the main street that ran parallel to King Creek. It was typical of a hundred others he had passed through. Saloons, saddlers, meat purveyors and general stores mingled with more specialied premises such as a sweet shop for the kids and tobacconists for their fathers. There was even a furniture store, a large double fronted emporium that was taking advantage of the local raw material.

The most prosperous structures in the centre of the town boasted ornately carved false fronts painted in various colours. The majority, however, were little more than shacks. The town had clearly still to establish itself as a prosperous centre for trade.

Brady drew his mount to a halt outside the one place where he was sure to obtain the information he required. Still embracing the old glory days, the Miners' Haven must have been one of the first buildings to be erected. It occupied a central position fronting a plaza.

Tying off, Cheyenne stepped up on to the boardwalk and entered the saloon through its swing doors. It was early afternoon. The dim interior was lit by a couple of smelly tallow lamps.

Business was quite brisk for that time of day. In addition to numerous drinkers, a pianist was practising a new number over near a small stage at the back.

Lazing at a green baize table, a gambler sporting a garish vest and natty pork pie hat idly played patience. Nobody had yet availed themselves of his leery patter to get rich quick. A languid peeper studied the newcomer assessing him as a potential client. But Cheyenne Brady had more important issues on his mind than gambling.

He sidled up to the bar and ordered a beer. Two cowboys in range gear were huddled over their drinks. They casually eyed the newcomer.

'Ridden far?' the older one enquired noting Cheyenne's dust-stained appearance. Judd Fargo was the ramrod for the Broken Wheel horse ranch. His sidekick was a young 'puncher calling himself Idaho Blue. They had come to Jackpot to sell a pair of stallions to the owner of the Miners' Haven.

'Just come in off the Black Rock,' Cheyenne replied. 'Sure is a dry spot.' He tossed back his head imbibing the cool beer with relish.

'Heading far?' Blue asked.

Cheyenne couldn't suppress a grin. This pair were like a variety act.

Blue noticed the lopsided smirk and balked at the new-comer's attitude. He squared off, hands dropping to curl menacingly above the handles of his twin-rigged gunbelt. 'You gotten a beef agin us, mister, cos I don't cotton to your attitude?'

'Easy there, kid,' advised Idaho Blue's associate. 'The guy don't mean nothing. He just forgot to hang a right outside town.' The ramrod shot a bleak eye towards the feathers in Brady's hat before finishing with a sarcastic jibe, 'You *were* lookin' to meet up with your redskin buddies at the Shoshone camp, weren't you, fella?'

The piano player stopped playing, likewise the gambler shuffling his cards. Here was a far more interesting scenario about to unfold. Even the house cat stumbled to a halt, the mouse it had been pursuing forgotten. The rest of the clientele followed their lead. Time hung heavier than a chunk of lead inside the fetid atmosphere of the saloon.

Cheyenne sighed in resignation. Here we go again, he thought. Some knuckleheads just couldn't leave his Indian heritage alone.

The older dude should have known better. And here was yet another young tearaway sporting the hardware he assumed would change him into a tough hardcase. In any other circumstances, Cheyenne would have taught both cowpunchers a lesson. But he didn't want any trouble. A far more important quarry was in his sights.

So he held up his hands to placate the irate hothead.

'My mistake, kid, I didn't mean nothing. Just thinking about something else, is all.'

He turned away to finish his drink figuring that the incident was over. But Idaho Blue was riled up and itching to try out his new bone-handled Colt .45s. He had saved up his meagre wages for six months to buy them. The over-indulgence of liquor he had imbibed only served to exacerbate his surly mood.

'Backing down like a spineless rat, are yuh?' snarled the kid flexing his fingers urgently. 'Well I'm calling you out. Go for your gun, yellow belly.'

Cheyenne appealed to the older man to control his rabid associate. 'You need to keep a muzzle on this crazy mutt,' he rasped. 'The kid should still be in school.' But the petition came out more as a slur against the ramrod's authority.

Fargo snarled out a caustic grunt then stepped away from the bar.

'You heard what Idaho said. Either eat humble pie and

crawl out of here on your belly, or use that hogleg.' He aimed a lump of spit at Cheyenne's boots. The slimy gloop slid down the leather. 'Maybe it's just sitting there for show to impress the ladies. Not that any respectable woman would speak to a stinking half-breed.'

Without waiting for any further insults to come his way, Cheyenne whipped out his revolver and slugged the kid over the head. Idaho Blue was caught on the hop. His hands hadn't even touched the shiny butts of his new guns. The young cowpoke slumped to the floor. Out for the count, his hat had thankfully prevented any serious damage.

Cheyenne's own gun then swept round to prod the ramrod's grubby neck.

'I said that I didn't want any trouble, and that's what I meant,' he hissed into the guy's ear. 'I have bigger fish to fry than you pair of dung heaps. Now get this hothead out of here before I get angry.'

'S-sure, mister,' stuttered Judd Fargo hoisting up the young cowpoke. 'Guess we got to holding the wrong end of the stick.'

'You sure did,' Brady rapped turning away to finish his drink in peace. 'And for your information, I'm Cheyenne, Cheyenne Brady. Remember that when folks ask who stuck a burr up your asses. Now git!'

A narrowed gaze followed the two rannies, making sure they left the saloon. Then he turned his attention back to the gaping bartender. The incident with the two Broken Wheel hands had happened so fast that the guy had barely been given time to blink.

'Has another young punk called in here recently? He's

got straggly blond hair,' Brady enquired, pushing his glass across the bar for a refill.

'We get plenty of them passing through here,' the bartender shrugged.

'This one likes to think he's another Wild Bill Hickok.'

Mention of the celebrated gunslinging lawman jerked the 'keep from his reverie. He filled up the pot and pushed it back. 'On the house,' he muttered when Cheyenne offered to pay. 'Those guys were asking for trouble. Been drinking all afternoon. You sure clammed 'em up good. Ain't seen action like that since Dirty Dan Bowder strung a cheating tinhorn up on the rafters by his suspenders. Boy, that was some sight to behold.'

Cheyenne was more interested in his own affairs.

'This dude calls himself Kid Syrillo. You seen him?' he persisted, encouraging the barman to concentrate on this more urgent matter.

Egghead Johnny Viper scratched his bald pate in thought. Then he nodded. 'Don't know his handle. But a young strutter just like Wild Bill stopped off here a couple of days back. He only stayed long enough for a couple of drinks. Although he did ask for the quickest way to reach the Oregon border.'

Cheyenne's face lit up. So he was on the right trail.

'Is he a friend of your'n?' asked Egghead.

'We're acquainted.' The response was briskly concise. He didn't want to give anything else away. 'Maybe you could give me the same directions.'

'Sure thing.' The barman then went on to outline the route taken by Kid Syrillo. But he added an extra piece of welcome information. 'If'n you want to catch him up, there's a short cut over the Granite Range through Alkali Pass. Taking that will cut two days off your journey.' Cheyenne perked up even more on hearing this. 'You could be in the border town of Denio to meet him. Now wouldn't that be a pleasant surprise?'

'It sure would,' grinned Cheyenne. But not in the way you're figuring, mister. Although he kept that notion to himself. Egghead Johnny then went on to describe the route to be followed.

After finishing his drink, Cheyenne thanked the helpful barman and left the saloon. Delving into his pockets, he was disturbed to find only a few dollars left.

The flight from Winnemucca had left him high and dry. The dough was only just enough to stock up on the most basic of provisions, beans, fatback and beef jerky, not forgetting the all-important coffee. That would have to see him through the next stage of his quest for vengeance.

It was late afternoon when Cheyenne left Jackpot. Heading north west towards the Oregon border, he reckoned on a couple of hours before he needed to make camp. He had been riding for no more than one of those when the dipping sun reflected off what could only be metal. It came from in amongst some rocks up ahead on the right of the trail.

There it was again.

Crinkling eyebrows puckered in a frown. What could it be out here in the wilderness?

Then it struck him: a gun barrel! Those two feisty rannigans must be lying in wait. And their intentions were clear as a church bell – to finish off their fracas permanently. But what to do about it? He would presently come within range of the waiting long guns. Gradually, he eased the sorrel down to a steady trot so as not to alert the bushwhackers to the fact that he had spotted them.

Knowing their exact location was a distinct advantage. The small copse of trees just ahead was the answer to his dilemma. Momentarily, he would be hidden from view. That would allow him to swing off the trail and surprise them from behind.

Once in the tree cover, he dismounted and moved in amongst the cluster of rocks. Keeping out of sight, he quickly gained height moving quietly through the amalgam of stones careful not to make any noise. Occasional pauses were made to keep track of his position and that of his quarry. Time was of the essence. Any moment now, they would realize that something had gone wrong when he did not emerge from the trees.

Seconds later, he spotted the black hat of Judd Fargo. His young buddy was close by and had clearly recovered from the pistol whipping. Cheyenne edged closer, purposefully avoiding the thorny cat claw and mesquite bushes that reached out to snare his clothing. Revolver palmed, he made ready to confront the bushwhacking duo.

The two men were concentrating all their attention on the trail below. Blue stood up trying to obtain a better look.

'See anything?' The anxious query from Judd Fargo easily reached Cheyenne's ears.

Blue shook his head. 'Where in thunder is he? The rat should have appeared by now.'

'You guys are looking in the wrong place.'

That sudden gritty announcement caught the inept pair off guard. Idaho Blue almost tumbled over the edge of the rock over which he was leaning. Fargo quickly recovered. He swing to face the surprise appearance of their prey.

Cheyenne pre-empted the guy's intention to even the score. 'That carbine moves any further and you're heading for the high plains, mister.' The death threat rattled out with a brusque snap. It was backed up by the prodding revolver.

Fargo hesitated. Then he thought better of making any rash move. The gun was lowered.

'You made the right choice, fella.'

But Idaho had no such compunctions. This jasper had shamed him in front of an audience. And now he was threatening to do it all over again. That was asking too much of a hot-tempered rannie like Idaho Blue. The consequences of backing down now didn't occur to him. All he could see was a red mist floating before his eyes. And there in the blurry haze stood the all-consuming figure of that lowlife half-breed taunting him to make use of his new guns.

In truth, the last thing Brady wanted was a gunfight with these two stubborn clowns. But he was given no choice in the matter.

'Don't do it, Blue!'

Even the yell from his buddy to see sense failed to stall the kid's stampede to hell and damnation.

Blue snarled like a rabid puma, grabbing for his bone-handled Colts. The guns lifted, swung upwards. But that was as far as they got. Flame lanced from the barrel of

105

Cheyenne's pistol slamming the critter back. Head over heels, the single bullet punched him back off the cliff edge. The pistol scythed round to cover his partner. Blue eyes warned of a similar fate should the ramrod choose to try his own luck.

Fargo was far more circumspect. His hands lifted in surrender.

'He asked for that,' Brady said, anxious to make certain the ramrod would back up his plea of self-defence when the local lawdog was informed. 'I was given no choice.'

Judd Fargo agreed. 'It was bound to happen sometime. He'd been practicing with those new guns all week. Rabbits and varmints just weren't enough for the durned fool. Now he's paid the price.'

'You make certain the law knows about that cos I ain't got the time to hang around.'

'Sorry about that Indian jibe,' Fargo said with evident remorse. 'It was a cheap shot.'

Cheyenne did not disagree. He merely gave a curt nod acknowledging the apology. Then he indicated for the man to lead the way back down through the scattering of boulders. They both assisted in slinging Idaho's body over the cowpoke's horse.

'The kid won't mind if'n I take his rifle. He won't be needing it, but I sure do.'

Just to be on the safe side, he watched Judd Fargo make his way back towards Jackpot leading the dead man's horse. He stuck around for another ten minutes in case the ramrod had a change of heart and decided to avenge his young associate. But nobody appeared. The message had clearly got through: you mess with Cheyenne Brady at your cost.

Kid Syrillo was also going to discover the veritable truth of that proposition.

TEN

GARY CALLS THE SHOTS

Cheyenne reached the border as the sun was nearing its zenith. A rotting signboard, the red paint faded and barely legible, was all there was to inform travellers they were now entering the state of Oregon. If'n that bald-headed saloon Johnny was correct, then he ought to have arrived here ahead of the Kid.

Cheyenne settled down behind a cluster of rocks. He had a clear view of his back trail for a mile or more. Enough time to ready himself for greeting the cocky braggart. His reckoning was that Syrillo should pass by sometime before nightfall. At least that was the hope. In crossing the border into his home state, Cheyenne was counting on the Kid relaxing his vigilance thinking he had thrown off any pursuit.

It was four o'clock when a rider hove into view.

Cheyenne narrowed his eyes focusing on the approaching horseman. A mirthless smile cracked the grim façade. There was no mistaking that arrogant posture. The lank wisps of straw hair were lit up by the late afternoon sun. Positioning himself behind the Joshua tree on which the border sign was nailed he waited for the inevitable show-down.

The Winchester carbine apprehended from Idaho Blue rested in the crook of his arm.

The Kid had spotted the sign, but not the man concealed behind it. He drew his mount to a halt. 'Made it home!' he muttered into the horse's ear, giving the animal's head a friendly rub.

'Not quite, Kid,' came the stark assertion as Brady stepped out into the open. 'You have to ride pass me to enter Oregon. And I ain't about to let that happen.' The gun swung to cover the stunned rider.

Syrillo's mouth fell open. He could barely credit that his old adversary had somehow managed to outwit him. He shook his head thinking a ghost from the past had come back to haunt him. But the bastard was still there.

This was for real, no nightmarish figment of his imagination.

'I'm prepared to give you an even break, Kid,' Brady rasped out cranking his rifle. 'That's a sight more than you gave me back in Emigrant Pass.' Recall of the heinous act brought a sour twist to Brady's mouth. 'Now get down off'n that cayuse and we'll do this properly, man to man like it should be. Figure you're up to that . . . back-shooter?' The final word was spat out with venomous intent.

The Kid's hand moved towards his holstered revolver.

'Any devious tricks and I'll blast you out of that saddle without a second's thought.' The staccato jab halted the Kid's sly manoeuvring. 'Now step down slow and easy on this side and move out into the open where I can see your mangy hide.'

Syrillo snarled, but he had no option but to comply.

Keeping a wary eye on his opponent, Cheyenne carefully placed his rifle against a rock.

'Now it's just you and me, Kid.' The statement was flat and devoid of emotion. 'Winner takes all.'

'How did you track me down?' Syrillo growled morosely.

Cheyenne laughed. 'You should have looked in the mirror. Then you'd know.'

The Kid frowned.

'That Hickok look is a dead giveaway, Kid. A herd of Texas longhorns couldn't have left a more obvious trail to follow.' The droll twinkle in his blue eyes suddenly froze to a hard glint of ice as he recalled what he was here for. 'Too late for that now. Unless of course you strike it lucky and come out of this with a whole skin.'

A languid hand pointed to a inquisitive prairie dog that was perched on a rock watching the strange events unfold.

'When that little guy gets fed up and shifts his ass, that's when we go to shooting. But not before.' Cheyenne knew that he had the edge. Patience was not one of the Kid's strong points. And the longer the gopher stood there, the more fidgety he would become. 'So that's two things you have to watch. Me and Gary the Gopher. It could be for a minute or half an hour. But we wait until that critter decides our fate.'

Seconds became minutes. And still the little gopher had not deigned to make a move. His beady eyes had flicked between the two strange beings, questioning what was taking place within his domain. But innate curiosity kept him riveted to the spot.

A film of sweat broke across Syrillo's face. He was feeling the strain. Cheyenne knew what would happen if Gary did not disappear soon.

And so it came to pass.

The Kid snarled, his frustration boiling over. A hand grabbed for the pistol on his hip. It appeared to jump into his hand and begin shooting.

He was fast. No doubt about it. Leaden death poured forth searching for the body of Cheyenne Brady. But the half-breed was ready for the illicit ploy. He threw himself to one side while palming his own gun. The Kid's bullets whistled harmlessly past his ear. Close, but not close enough.

Not so Cheyenne's own response. Two bullets ripped into the Kid's chest. Both were killing shots. A bright red flood discharged from the flapping mouth. Syrillo slumped to his knees before keeling over.

The gopher scampered away having unwittingly played a deadly part in the grim proceedings.

Cheyenne strolled across to the still body, the instrument of death hanging down by his side. Tendrils of smoke dribbled from the barrel. He stared down at the corpse and shook his head. There was no feeling of elation etched across the stark features. Only a twinge of regret that he had been the reluctant harbinger of the young

111

guy's demise.

But it was only brief. Kid Syrillo had been a willing participant in his own destiny. And his body was worth a sight more than the bounty offered by the Nevada law authorities. It would be his endorsement for acceptance back into the gang. Rafe Culpepper had no clemency towards those who ran out on him.

There was that time a year back when Smoke Tacoma ran away from a violent gun battle with the posse out of Eureka Springs.

Led by a stalwart lawman going under the gaudy handle of Rainbow Ross Tavener, the posse had run the gang to ground in a box canyon in the Toquima Range. It didn't matter a jot to the florid-featured tinstar that it was over the border in Utah where he had no jurisdiction.

Tavener was not giving up. His son, and deputy town marshal, had been killed during the messy bank heist. During the dogged pursuit, the lawdog's white hat and distinctively coloured vest were like a thorn in the gang's side. Tacoma had panicked when the gang made a stand against their determined pursuers. Sneaking off during the gunfight, his disappearance was only noticed when Culpepper had managed to effect an escape during the hours of darkness.

The next month was spent scouring all the known flesh-pots in which a rat like Smoke Tacoma was likely to seek solace. He was eventually run to ground in the Nevada mining camp of Virginia City. The bullet-riddled corpse was strung up to a cottonwood. Pinned to the victim's chest was a sign that read: *A quitter who abandoned his buddies.*

With the Kid's body securely strapped over his saddle, Cheyenne turned around and headed back towards his meeting with old Sourdough Lamar in Stonewall Flats. Cheyenne was concerned that Sheriff Pershing had a reputation similar to that of Rainbow Ross. The Winnemucca lawman would try his darnedest to hunt down the Blackjacks now that they had besmirched his town. Consequently, he was forced to make a wide detour south through the Stillwater Mountains to avoid any chance of running into any posse. He was, therefore, later arriving at Stonewall Flats than expected. But better safe than sorry.

As expected, Sourdough was propping up the bar in the Esmeralda Saloon. The old timer was regaling a captive audience with a lively selection of tall stories about his gaudy prospecting life. Although Lamar embellished his adventures with bizarre fabrications intended to spice them up, there was no doubting that he told a good yarn.

Cheyenne hung back listening in wonder to some rich incidents that had his audience enthralled. After delivering the final crescendo, a round of hearty applause broke out. It was no surprise that Sourdough's rousing performance earned him numerous free drinks.

But there was one guy who had seen through the old-timer's game. A big jasper with black hair and an even blacker moustache pushed through the crowd to confront the raconteur.

'You're a durned liar, mister,' he rasped, rolling back on his heels. Duke Winston was drunk as a skunk. But he still recognized a blatant tall story when he heard one. 'Nobody could have survived that and lived to tell the tale.'

113

Not again, sighed Cheyenne. He had been here once before after the pair of them had been released from Greystoke and walked into Virginia City. On that occasion it had been Lamar's innate friendliness that had gotten him into trouble. Now it was his garrulous manner.

Winston pushed the older man in the chest. 'Seems like it's you that should be buying the drinks for cheating all these brainless saps.'

'Who you calling a sap?' complained a man leaning on the bar.

'Well if'n you believe this knucklehead, you're more of a fool than he is.'

'Don't you be calling my partner a fool,' came the caustic admonition from another drinker.

In no time at all, the whole saloon erupted as men began throwing punches at one another. The fracas rapidly spread as chairs and tables were upended and flung about. No amount of pleading and threats from the bartender had any effect. His panic-stricken entreaties went unheard amidst the frenetic mêlée.

Cheyenne was forced to duck as a chair leg sailed past his head. Desperately he scanned the room searching for his partner. At that moment, Sourdough appeared from beneath a table where he had taken refuge.

'Am I glad to see you, old buddy,' he said, covering his head to avoid a flying table. 'Why is it that some folks just don't enjoy a good story?'

Cheyenne ignored the question as a bottle came winging across the battleground. It shattered against the wall showering them both with fragments. He shook his head in wonder, grateful to have avoided injury.

114

'Let's get out of here before the realization hits that they've all been fooled,' he urged crawling towards the door.

'What do you mean, boy?' grumbled the old guy somewhat piqued at having his veracity queried. 'My stories ain't made up. They are all the real thing.'

'And the moon's made of green cheese,' chuckled Brady, urging his partner forward. 'Now let's get out of here.'

Scrambling under the batwings, they both lurched to their feet and hurried away while they were still able.

Two blocks west and on the adjoining street, the two amigos paused to get their breath. They could still hear the uproar emanating from the Esmeralda. Both men grinned at each other.

'You sure know how to keep a fella on his toes,' declared Brady shaking his head in bewilderment.

'It helps to keep me young,' replied Sourdough, matching his partner's wide grin. 'I never could have settled down to a routine life where nothing happens to stir a guy's blood except the next payment of his mortgage.'

Brady couldn't help but agree with that supposition. 'So where have you been staying while I've been away?' he enquired.

'The local livery man allowed me to occupy a stall in exchange for helping out,' replied Sourdough, although he was more interested in his partner's adventures. 'So did you catch up with the Kid?'

'I left the skunk back yonder.' Brady flicked his head in the general direction of the hills to the north of town. 'I'm camped out in a draw off the main trail.'

'I trust you have him hogtied and gagged.'

'Don't need a gag,' replied Brady. 'He ain't gonna be doing no more jawing.'

'You mean—?'

Brady pre-empted the obvious assumption. 'With the help of a friendly bartender in Jackpot, I managed to reach the Oregon border ahead of him. He had the chance to walk away from an even-handed showdown. But like the two-faced rat that he was, the Kid tried to pull a lowdown stunt.'

'What did he do?' Sourdough was all agog to hear the story.

Cheyenne shrugged. 'He drew before his time. It came as no surprise. And he lost.'

'So what happens now?' asked Sourdough.

'We head for Gabbs Hole and keep our fingers crossed that Big-Nose Rafe is appeased enough let us join up when he sees that I've brought the Kid in.'

By this time they had reached the livery stable. The ostler was peering up the street. 'What's all that ruckus up at the Esmeralda?' the little guy asked.

Both men looked to their rear following the ostler's baffled gaze. Their eyes lifted in astonishment as a chair crashed through the saloon's front window.

'There's always some guys wanting to cause trouble,' averred Brady clicking his tongue in a mocking rebuke.

'The marshal oughta lock them up and throw away the key,' added Sourdough with a wry wink at his partner.

The ostler gave a vigorous nod of agreement.

'Guess I'll be pulling out now, Homer,' Lamar said entering the stable to retrieve his horse. 'Much obliged for

116

the shakedown.'

Homer Tubbs shook a vague hand in acknowledgement. All his attention was focused on the hubbub at the Esmeralda. The fight had now poured out on to the street.

The main instigator of the fracas along with his partner made a swift exit from Stonewall Flats before the truth dawned.

ELEVEN

INCIDENT AT WHITEHORSE BUTTE

Well before they reached their destination, Cheyenne was having second thoughts about rejoining the Blackjacks. The more he mulled it over and the closer they got to Gabbs Hole, the greater became his doubts. Rafe Culpepper was not a man to forgive easily.

Bringing back the Kid might appease him. But there was still the matter of having set up the potential trap in Winnemucca. Would he be so forbearing when it came to overlooking such a betrayal? Cheyenne was rapidly arriving at the conclusion that he would not.

That had been a slap in the face for which the gang leader would want redress.

But there was another issue at stake that was far more

important as far as Cheyenne was concerned. If he joined up with Culpepper and things went awry, his burgeoning relationship with Jody Dunstan would be soured for ever. There could be no going back.

He dragged his horse to a halt. A serious frown creased his worried brow. A loping jack rabbit gave the two men a startled glance as it shot across the trail and disappeared into a clutch of beaver tails.

There was another way out of this dilemma.

Sourdough had picked up on his partner's gloomy mood some time back. For the last half-hour not a word had been spoken.

'Some'n is bugging you,' he submitted tentatively. Pre-empting a response to the blunt remark, he voiced the thought that had been nagging at his own view of their situation. 'You certain this is what you want, boy? I'll go along with shopping the gang for your sake and because we're partners, but somehow it don't sit right. I ain't no squealer. Never have been.'

Cheyenne knew this hesitation on the part of his associate needed clearing up.

'Make no mistake,' he stressed fixing a trenchant eye on his partner, 'those guys are mean critters. They didn't think twice about robbing the bank in Winnemucca where all our savings and those of the other townsfolk were being held. Blackjacks is a name that fits them to a T. Anybody gets in their way and they'll shoot 'em down without a second's hesitiation. And that includes the two of us.

'We've both been tarred with the same brush. And, as things stand, we're no better in the eyes of the law. Join up with the Blackjacks and we'll likely end up as crow bait.'

'You've sure changed your tune,' Lamar said rather curtly.

A tear dribbled from the corner of his partner's right eye.

Lamar knew that he was thinking of Jody Dunstan.

Brady coughed to hide the catch in his voice before adding, 'You claim to have been railroaded by that double-crossing partner who stole your poke. So you ain't no hard-boiled owlhoot on the prod. That right?'

'Guess so,' Lamar said thoughtfully. 'I hadn't thought about it like that afore.'

Cheyenne paused to consider his final declaration. 'We both worked durned hard for that dough and were building up a solid business to be proud of. But if'n you want to end up on boot hill or spend the rest of your life in the pokey, then we should part company here and now. But I aim to bring those guys down, whatever the cost.'

'So what are you proposing we do about it?'

Confusion was etched across Lamar's leathery features.

'I reckon we should head for Winnemucca and persuade the sheriff that we're on the level,' Cheyenne said with conviction. 'Bringing in the body of the Kid will score in our favour. And Gabe Pershing is a fair-minded guy. He'll do the right thing.'

The old guy was not so sure. He would rather they just rode away and started up some place where nobody knew them. Back into the Black Hills country perhaps.

'What about that skunk of a mayor?' he countered sceptically. 'Him and those other council dudes won't be so easy to bring round.'

'I didn't say it would be simple. But we've a sight more chance of coming out of this on the right side than if'n we head for Gabbs Hole. I'm convinced of that now. Our only choice lies in persuading the sheriff to mount a posse to raid the gang's hideout. And I'm the only one who knows the way in.'

Lamar shrugged, then nodded slowly. Reluctantly he agreed to go along with his partner's suggestion. 'Can't say that I'm over keen on going back there. But whatever you decide, I'll support you all the way.'

'I know you will, Sourdough.' Brady's voiced softened. 'It's the right thing to do if'n we're going to clear our names. No way am I going back to Greystoke.'

'That makes two of us, pard,' averred the old jasper clawing a hand through his grizzled beard. Then a fresh twinkle gleamed in his eye, 'Let's hope you have the gift of the gab to persuade all them critters that you're on the level.'

Turning away from the Monte Cristo range, they headed north towards Winnemucca.

Cheyenne's hurried departure from the town had been reported in the *Virginia Epitaph*. Indeed it was front page news. To Rafe Culpepper, having his old associate accused of being still tied in with the Blackjacks was cause for much joviality. It also came as a welcome relief. Now that the turncoat had been unceremoniously forced into fleeing Winnemucca, there was no need for the gang to quit Nevada and their favoured hideout of Gabbs Hole.

Those two-bit pen-pushers and store johnnies had gotten the better of him by stymying the bank raid. That was a humiliating climbdown for a proud jasper of Culpepper's ilk and something he could not allow to pass

121

unchallenged. Now that he felt safe with Brady on the run, he fully intended to teach those critters a lesson.

What he had in mind would unequivocally prove that the Blackjacks were still in business and not a force to be messed with. His cunning plan initially involved holding up the local stagecoach on the town's own doorstep.

It was only a ten mile stretch between Winnemucca and the town of Golconda. Nobody would expect it to be attacked. Maybe the proceeds would be meagre, but the kudos gained for Big-Nose Rafe and the gang together with the shock effect was worth the trouble.

So here they were secreted behind Whitehorse Butte. The lofty pinnacle was the only rocky excrescence between the two settlements. Elko Boon had taken up a position on the top of the crag to give warning of the stagecoach's approach. The others sat their mounts down below ready to ride out when the signal was given.

It was ten o'clock in the morning.

Culpepper kept a wary eye on the sentinel awaiting his signal.

'Check your hardware, boys, and mask up,' he spat out. 'Those varmints are about to get the surprise of their miserable lives.' The men quickly filled their hands and hid their faces.

Boon raised a hand. That was the signal to attack.

Culpepper dug his spurs into the bay's flanks. The big horse leapt forward out on to the trail in front of the coach. Supporting him was Mesa Quinn. Both men had their guns menacingly on show. High up on the rock ledge, Elko Boon loosed off a single shell from his Winchester. The bullet lifted the hat from the driver's head. It was a perfect shot intended to show that the gang meant business.

'Haul up there, mister,' growled Culpepper. 'This is a heist and you're being robbed by the Nevada Blackjacks.'

Windy Macaw and Jackknife Stringer pulled out behind the coach effectively cutting off any retreat.

'Now throw down that strong box. And no funny business,' rapped Culpepper.

Stinkweed Doolin complied without any hesitation. He was too stunned by the sudden assault to think of retaliating. And with so many guns pointing his way, discretion was most assuredly the safer option. The box hit the ground with a dull thud. His shotgun followed soon after.

'Open it up, Mesa,' the gang boss ordered. 'Let's see if'n this little business transaction was worth the effort.'

A couple of well-placed bullets blasted the heavy lock to smithereens. Quinn toed open the box. 'We've done a heap better than expected, boss,' he exclaimed gleefully hauling out a couple of heavy sacks which he shook. 'Sounds like gold nuggets too.'

'Lady Luck is sure watching over us, boys,' Culpepper hollered. Then, addressing the passengers inside the coach. 'Everybody out, folks. And remember who's holding the guns.'

On this trip there were only three passengers. They stepped down. Anxious looks clouded their pinched faces.

The two men were quickly frisked by Windy Macaw. None of them were carrying weapons. Mayor Wendover was on his way to Golconda to finalize a deal for the purchase of some land. He was accompanied by the storekeeper, Norbert Dench who was in on the deal.

Wendover had managed to arrange his meeting to coincide with that of the third passenger, a particularly attractive female whom he had been trying to cultivate on the brief journey. So far without any success.

He was the only one of the passengers who chose to voice any displeasure.

'This is outrageous,' snapped Wendover foaming at the mouth. His round face had turned a vibrant purple. 'I am the Mayor of Winnemucca. How dare you treat me like this. You won't get away with it.'

'Seems like we already have, mister,' chirped up Macaw grinning from ear to ear. The others joined in the hilarity much to Wendover's embarrassment. 'And I've taken a shine to them fancy new boots. Take them off!'

'And I'll have that sparkly watch and chain,' added Stringer.

'Tell you what,' interrupted Culpepper drawing his horse closer to the sweating official. He leaned forward and jabbed his gun into the quivering belly. 'You made a fool of the Blackjacks when we tried to rob the bank in Winnemucca, now it's your turn, fat boy.'

Wendover bristled with indignation. But it was all inept bluster that was ignored by the gang leader. 'Let's give this mouthy windbag a taste of what Governor Langhorn enjoyed on the Ruth copper mine heist. Strip the varmint down to his underwear then we can all see what he's made of.'

Wendover tried to remonstrate but the threatening pistol soon closed off any attempt at resistance. In no time he was left standing in nothing but a dingy pair of unsavoury long johns.

Dench stifled a smirk at his associate's distress. But he remained stoically quiet and escaped with merely having his possessions removed rather than his dignity.

Satisfied with his shaming of the mayor, Culpepper now turned his attention to the third passenger. Here was a far more attractive prospect than the pathetic figure of Amos Wendover.

'So what have you to offer us, miss?' the gang leader said, making an elaborate bow. A gleam of approval lit up his rugged features. 'A few baubles perhaps, or maybe some fine perfume to improve the smell of your associate here?' He laughed at the witticism as a languid hand swept over the red-faced mayor.

'I regret that I am but a poor traveller visiting a friend in the next town,' chirped the young woman exhibiting her most coy bearing. But inside, her whole persona was aquiver with fright. 'All I have in my purse are those discreet items that ladies need to keep themselves . . . erm, shall we say . . . fresh?'

Her nose twitched at the sorry specimen cowering on her right.

But the gang boss had lost interest.

'Say what you like, sister, I ain't really bothered. Now search her bag,' Culpepper snapped out gesturing for Macaw to resume his clumsy rummaging. Big-Nose Rafe's brief attempt at playing the considerate gentleman had come to a stumbling halt. 'We ain't got time to hang around here splitting the breeze.'

Mesa Quinn was also giving the woman more than a cursory appraisal. He had seen her somewhere before. And recently. Now where was it? His brow furrowed in concentration. Then it struck him like a rampant bear on the razzle.

He snapped his fingers.

That's right. She was walking down the main street of Winnemucca cosying up to Cheyenne Brady. And he had also seen her in the office of the bank manager while he was sussing out the joint.

'I know this little gal,' he said in a sly drawl. 'She's the bank manager's daughter. The one who's been walking out with Brady since he decided to sell us down the river.'

Culpepper's eyes gleamed on hearing this tasty morsel. A plan instantly began to form in his devious mind.

'You're coming with us, lady.' Jody's face turned white with dismay. 'She can double up with you, Jackknife.'

'My pleasure, boss,' leered the lean tough, grabbing hold of the woman who was too stunned to put up any show of resistance. His large paws lingered over the shapely form as he bundled her on to his horse.

'And you Mr Mayor,' hissed the gang leader spearing the anxious tub of lard with a malevolent stare, 'can inform the dame's father that he can have her back safe and sound in exchange for all that lovely dough sitting in the bank. I'll let him know when and where it's to be delivered in due course.' His next order was to the driver. 'Now swing this heap around and get back where you came from.'

A ribald halloo issued from his throat as he led the Blackjacks off in the direction of the Monte Cristos. The two remaining passengers were left grovelling about in the clouds of dust raised by stamping hoofs as the gang departed.

*

It was around the time that the stagecoach made its ignominious return to Winnemucca that Cheyenne Brady and
his partner were also approaching the town. Just by
chance, Brady chose to pause within the same cluster of
trees in which the Blackjacks had camped prior to their
fateful raid.

'I'm going in alone,' he announced, peering down
from the low hillock. At that moment the stagecoach thun-
dered into the town from the east. He paid it no heed.
Had he realized the significance of the unscheduled
arrival, indubitably his next steps would have been different. But that is how one's fate and destiny are determined.

'You sure that's wise?' queried a doubtful Lamar. 'I
don't trust those good citizens one bit. They're a bunch of
conniving chisellers.' There was an acrid bite to the
denunciation. 'No better than the Blackjacks if'n you ask
me.'

'You could be right, Sourdough,' agreed Cheyenne
evenly. 'That's why I don't want you involved more than is
necessary. If'n things do go wrong down there, you high-
tail out of here and don't look back.'

Lamar blustered indignantly. 'What d'you take me for,
boy? A durned yellow belly? I ain't leaving you to face this
alone then cutting loose like a frightened jack-rabbit when
the pot boils over. We're in this together. And that's the
goddamned end of the matter.'

No amount of cajoling would sway his partner. They
were a team as far as the old timer was concerned and
would go down fighting side by side if'n that was to be

127

their fate.

'In that case . . .' Cheyenne paused, musing over how best to formulate his plan. He still did not want to endanger the ex-miner unnecessarily. 'You stay up here and keep watch. If'n I fail to return by sundown, then you'll have to figure out what to do next. But there ain't no sense in the both of us heading down there to get arrested.' He shrugged off the old guy's misgivings. 'Not that it's going to happen. I'm confident of being able to persuade Pershing to form a posse to raid Gabbs Hole.'

Lamar allowed himself to be persuaded. But his dismal expression indicated his own view had not changed. They shook hands not knowing what the immediate future held.

TWELVE

ROOFTOP RESCUE

Cheyenne nudged his mount down the slope intending to approach the sheriff's office from the rear, just like the gang had done. He had not the slightest intimation of the furore about to be raised as the stagecoach rumbled down the main street.

Stinkweed Doolin jammed on the brake bringing the rattling conveyance bumping and skidding to a halt outside the Butterfield Agency.

Before the coach was given time to settle on its axles, Norbert Dench was out the door and racing up the street to his store. All queries from puzzled onlookers as to this uncharacteristic haste were brushed aside. Wendover had instructed his associate to procure some fresh duds from his store before he left the relative concealment of the coach's interior. The mayor had no intention of exposing himself to public ridicule.

'You should be in Golconda,' the agency clerk snapped

at the sweating driver. He tapped his watch. 'What in tarnation are you doing back here?'

'We were held up by the Blackjacks at Whitehorse Butte,' Doolin babbled out.

'How do you know it was them?' enquired Cabel Sankey who had come across from the Birdcage Hotel when he witnessed his friend hurrying up the street. If'n Norbert was running, something serious must have happened.

'The leader allus wears a copy of the skull and crossbones pinned to his hat,' asserted Stinkweed expounding his superior knowledge. 'And anyways, he told us. The guy wanted the mayor to know that it was his bunch that were involved.'

Before he was given time to explain further, the impatient clerk butted in. 'Did they get the strong box?'

'What do you think?' rapped the driver aiming a gob of spittle at his feet. 'But more important, they took Miss Jody hostage. They are holding her to ransom for the money they failed get on the raid against our bank.'

A crowd had gathered at the depot. It was not every day that incidents of this nature occurred in Winnemucca. Since the abortive heist by the Blackjacks, everybody had been on edge. A worried murmur broke out amongst the bystanders at this distressing news. Although if truth be told, it was the potential loss of their savings that troubled most folk.

Pushing through the crowd, the storekeeper thrust the procured garments through the window of the coach. He stood in front to conceal the incumbent while he quickly dressed. Gathering his dignity, the mayor stepped down, peered around in a lofty manner and addressed the crowd in his most stentorian voice.

'Make no mistake, folks, your cash is safe in the bank. And that's where it is staying.' A sigh of relief was released from numerous throats. 'Those thieving dogs will not get away with threatening this town. And any attempt by them to attack us again will be met with the fiercest opposition.'

With that he stamped across the street to report the hold-up to the sheriff who had just emerged from his office.

No mention at all had been made of the dire straits in which Jody Dunstan was being held. The fact that she could be killed if the gang's demands were not met appeared to have escaped the mayor's attention. It was left to the girl's father to enunciate his own anxiety in this regard.

'It is my daughter who has been kidnapped,' he stated frantically, tears welling in his eyes. 'And I am willing to surrender anything to secure her safe return.'

Members of the town council and other leading luminaries were gathered in the sheriff's office to discuss the traumatic events of the hold-up. Having been so emphatically humiliated by the Blackjacks, Wendover was in no mood for words of conciliation.

'You cannot expect the citizens of this town to surrender all their hard-earned money for the sake of one person.' Murmurs of agreement greeted this declaration by the odious official. Among them, much to Josiah Dunstan's chagrin, were those whom he had counted as friends. 'I have the whole hearted backing of the council in resisting any attempt to bargain with these outlaws.'

'Not from me you haven't,' shouted Dunstan. 'And

what is your ruling, Sheriff?' he said appealing to the lawman's integrity. 'Surely you cannot condone such a pitiless disregard for human life.'

Pershing held up his hands. 'I am just a paid official, Mr Dunstan,' he vacillated, even though his sympathies were with the distraught banker. 'If'n the majority refuse to deal with these felons, then my hands are tied.'

That was the moment when a subdued knock came on the cellblock door at the rear.

Pershing excused himself and went to open it. His mouth dropped open on seeing the figure of Cheyenne Brady standing there. With the sun at his back, the dark silhouette presented a sinister and menacing presence.

Totally unaware of the rumpus caused by the Whitehorse hold-up, the newcomer artlessly explained his presence. 'I've brought in the body of Kid Syrillo to prove that I ain't in cahoots with the Blackjacks,' he began. 'All I want is to—'

That was as far as he got. Pershing dragged out his revolver and pulled the startled visitor into the jail. Without any explanation, Cheyenne was roughly bundled into a vacant cell and the door was slammed shut. Its grim echo brought the other visitors scurrying into the narrow corridor. A key grating in the rusty lock had effectively imprisoned the reformed owlhoot whose naïve assumption of fairplay had been unequivocally shot to pieces.

'What's this all about?' complained Cheyenne gripping the cell bars. 'I came back here willingly to clear my name. All I want is help to break up the Blackjacks and then live peaceable like any other law-abiding citizen.' He appealed to Pershing as a solid upholder of truth and decency. 'You must know that I have never been in cahoots with the gang since arriving here to set up in business.'

But it was Amos Wendover who was in charge now. And he was having none of it.

'You are in league with those brigands and will stay here until we've caught every last one of them. I have no doubt that it was your scheming chicanery that led to the hold-up at Whitehorse Butte and the kidnapping of Miss Dunstan.'

On hearing this awful revelation, Cheyenne was lost for words. It was left to the impassioned mayor to sneeringly enlighten him. The mayor's brutal rendition bit deep into the prisoner's very soul.

'But if'n you call Rafe Culpepper's bluff, he'll kill the girl,' the captive remonstrated, slamming a fist on the iron bars of the cell. 'You can't be so ruthless as to allow that to happen. No amount of dough is worth that kind of sacrifice.'

Wendover brushed aside his protestations.'When the skunk realizes the town is not going to give in to his demands he'll release her then slink away like the coward he is. We are not going to let a bunch of outlaws dictate to us, are we, boys?' he berated loudly, appealing to the men who had crowded into the corridor behind him.

Nods and grunts of accord greeted the mayor's blunt stance. After hurling a few choice epithets in Cheyenne's direction, the gathering dispersed.

Only Josiah Dunstan had voiced his dissent at the heinous decision to abandon his daughter to her fate. But it had no effect. He had been noisily overruled by the more vociferous members of the council. The distraught banker stumbled away, a wretched grimace clouding his ashen features.

Cheyenne slumped down on to the grubby cot. He was in similar dismal straits. Head in hands he cursed his naïve stupidity at not listening to his old buddy's words of wisdom. Had they gone direct to Gabbs Hole, he could at least have found some way to extricate the girl from the gang's clutches.

Now he was truly in the mire, right up to his stiff, mule-headed neck.

The cellblock door slammed shut leaving the prisoner to miserably contemplate his desperate situation alone.

Slumped in his chair in the front office, Sheriff Pershing was once again obliged to organize protection for the town's financial resources. He took out a bottle of whiskey and imbibed a large slug. And this time when the Blackjacks hit the town, they would be extra vigilant to avoid being hoodwinked. He also felt ashamed at having bowed to Wendover's bluster.

Pershing was convinced that Big-Nose Rafe would not merely shrug his shoulders and ride away when he learned that the expected ransom demand had been refused. The gang boss would be madder than an angry sidewinder.

The blood ran cold in the lawman's veins at the thought. They might even decide to burn the place down. That notion didn't bear thinking on. That crazy mayor had gotten the town all fired up and there was nothing he could do about it.

Pershing shivered again. He was getting a mite too old for these sorts of predicaments.

Winnemucca had once been a quiet backwater where

the most excitement he could encounter was rolling the odd drunken cowpoke on a Saturday night. Now it felt like he was in the middle of a combat zone. It strongly reminded him of the war. But then he had been a lot younger and fighting for a cause in which he staunchly believed.

When the next election came round, Gabe Pershing intended standing down. It was a heap safer. He acknowledged now that he was no Wyatt Earp. But until then he was still sheriff and had a duty to uphold the law.

Up on the knoll outside town, old Sourdough was becoming more and more worried. There had been a hollow feeling in his stomach from the moment his stubborn young partner had left to stick his hand in the fire. Lamar was convinced that Cheyenne's optimism in persuading the town that he was on the level was foolhardy.

As the shadows lengthened, he gained no joy from being proved right. But what to do about it? Racking his brains for an answer to the dilemma, he finally latched on to a plan that might work. But it would have to be completed under the cloak of darkness.

Not until the last remnants of day had sunk behind the serated rim of the mountains did he make a move. Midnight had come and gone when he nudged his mount down the slope. Thankfully there was a full moon overhead to light his way. It would also enable his mission to be that much easier to complete successfully.

The key was the fact that the jailhouse was constructed of wood. Had it been of brick or adobe, what he had mind would prove impossible. A new more solidly constructed jailhouse had been suggested. But so far the funds had not been forthcoming. The bank was the only brick building in the town.

He located Cheyenne's sorrel at the back of the jail, proof that his buddy was still inside and being held captive. Backing off, Lamar entered the same derelict building used by Mesa Quinn during his spying mission for the Blackjacks. Taking care not to dislodge any loose boards, Lamar climbed on to the flat roof.

A probing eye scanned the street below. But it was midweek and the town had settled down for the night. He catfooted along to the edge below which ran a narrow alley. A short jump of no more than three feet brought him out on to the roof of the barber's shop. He knew that Cut-throat Carter did not live in the room above his salon which was merely used as a store, so there was no chance of disturbing anybody.

A couple more lock-ups were negotiated with ease.

The next obstacle to be overcome was the descent on to the roof of the jail. The cellblock behind the sheriff's office was a flat single storey structure with a weather-proofed tarpaulin covering the plank roof. Lowering his thin wiry frame over the rear edge of the barber's, he tested the drain pipe to ensure it was securely pinioned to the wall. A loose piece of wooden coping was accidently dislodged. It plunged into the alley below.

The clatter disturbed a cat that screeched loud enough to wake the dead. The animal shot beneath the building and disappeared. Lamar ducked out of sight. He held his breath, heart pounding in his chest, waiting for somebody to emerge from the jail. But all remained silent.

Luckily the pipe had plenty of projections to support his boots. Scrambling down it, he stretched a leg towards the edge of the cellblock roof. With one hand gripping the edge of the second storey, he levered himself carefully across.

This was where things became tricky. If the sheriff occupied the back room, he could be in serious trouble. All it needed was for the lawman to hear him at work on the roof and look out the window. That would be the end of his rescue bid.

The back window was half open. Lamar gingerly peered into the room. There was a bed but no sign of the sheriff. It must be a spare room unless he was still working down in his office. He would soon find out if'n the door opened and a light appeared. Until then he could set to work digging out a hole.

But first he need to learn if indeed Cheyenne was incarcerated below. He leaned over the edge of the roof above the barred window to one of the cells.

'You down there, Cheyenne?' he croaked out as quietly as possible.

A shuffling informed him that his buddy had heard. 'That you, Sourdough?' came back the animated response.

'Sure is.'

'Am I glad you came.' The relief at hearing a friendly voice was palpable.

'I'm going to dig a hole out from up here with my Bowie,' the prospector informed his buddy. 'Have you anything to help out from your side?'

'The sheriff never bothered to collect my supper things so I have a knife and fork in here.'

'Is he still out front in the office?' enquired the anxious rescuer.

'No,' hissed the prisoner. 'He went to bed over an hour ago.' Sourdough breathed a sigh of relief. That meant he had to be asleep in the front bedroom.

'Then let's get started,' Lamar urged. 'But keep the noise down.'

For the next half-hour they each carved and cut at the wooden roof. The tarpaulin covering was old and rotten which had allowed rainwater to soften the wood beneath. This considerably eased the task of widening a hole large enough for a man to climb through.

Lamar gave thanks to his Maker that the night was warm and the threatening rain storm had failed to materialize. By two o'clock, he was able to reach down and shake hands with his partner. Another half-hour passed before Cheyenne was able to scramble out on to the cell-block roof to join him.

The two men embraced. It was an emotional moment for them both. Sourdough in particular was most affected. He rubbed a tear from his eye.

'Thought I'd lost you there, boy,' he burbled gruffly trying to keep the catch from his voice. He had come to look on this young stalwart as the son he never had. Losing him would have been like losing a part of himself.

Cheyenne said nothing. He merely returned the sincere greeting with a warm smile. The brief moment was short lived. For there was no time to lose. They needed to be well away from the vicinity of Winnemucca before dawn.

The climb back across the rooftops was completed in

silence. Only when they were mounted and riding back up to the safety of the cottonwood knoll did Cheyenne express his grateful thanks for Lamar's bold rescue in words. At the same time, he was then able to inform his partner about the hold-up at Whitehorse Butte and the abduction of Jody Dunstan.

'It ain't no surprise to me that they still reckoned you were a member of the gang,' Lamar concluded after hearing the grim tidings. 'So what are we going to do about it?'

Cheyenne's brow furrowed. There was only one thing he could do.

An owl hooted somewhere out in the darkness. A bleak call of the predator with which Cheyenne Brady felt completely in tune.

They both rode out of the copse heading east in the direction of the Monte Cristos and Gabbs Hole.

THIRTEEN

SAWTOOTH CRACK

'We're getting close to the Hole.'

Cheyenne slowed the sorrel down to a walk. His nerves were on edge, strung tighter than a dancing girl's corset. He pointed out the tell-tale markings to Lamar which prevented those in the know from getting lost amidst the labyrinth of canyons. The old timer was impressed.

'No outsider would ever recognize those arrow signs as anything other than natural marks,' he endorsed. 'That Culpepper sure ain't wet behind the ears.'

'That's why we have to be mighty careful,' warned Cheyenne. 'He can smell a set-up before it's even been thought up. Another three miles along this trail and we'll be picking up an escort. Culpepper is sure to have posted a guard.'

No way would he be careless enough to reveal his presence, but the reformed outlaw knew where he was most likely to be concealed.

'So what's the plan you've been keeping under your hat since we left Winnemucca?'

Cheyenne had been loath to broach the scheme he had in mind in case it came to nothing. But now they were within striking distance of their goal, he saw no reason to keep his partner in the dark.

'See that rock up ahead that looks like an Indian's head?' Lamar nodded. 'Well, that's where we leave the trail and make our way around to the back of Gabbs Hole. All the gang's attention will be focused on this side in case Sheriff Pershing decides to mount an attack. Not that I think that's likely; he has no idea of the route through the canyons. But Culpepper is a wary cuss and won't be taking anything for granted.'

Upon reaching Indian Rock the pair stopped. Cheyenne dismounted and began searching for the sign that indicated the start of the little used track he was seeking. Just by chance, Lamar happened to glance behind. He was shocked to see a tiny plume of dust some half a mile on their back trail. It could only be from a rider who was following them.

'Hey, Cheyenne!' he called out, in a restrained though insistent hiss. 'There's some jasper on our tail.' He pointed behind him.

'Behind the rock!' his partner ordered, leading his own mount off the trail and out of sight.

Lamar joined him. They were none too soon either. A few minutes later, the rider appeared. He was completely oblivious to the fact he had been eyeballed. Only when the guy drew level did Cheyenne recognize him. And it came as another shock. He stepped out to halt the pursuer in his tracks.

'What in tarnation are you doing out here, Mr Dunstan?' he asked, holding on to the bridle of the banker's horse. Lamar stood to one side, a gun pointed at the banker.

Dunstan took a moment to let his heart settle following the abrupt challenge. 'When the sheriff informed the council you'd escaped through the jailhouse roof, I knew you'd go after the gang to rescue Jody.' His head dropped forward as the whole sorry episode flooded back. 'I had you all wrong, Cheyenne,' he muttered. 'And for that I profusely apologize.'

The banker shook off the despair that had enveloped him since learning of his daughter's abduction. A new resolve to fight for justice had injected starch into his backbone.

'It was the silver tongue of that freeloading mayor who had us all dancing to his tune,' he rasped. 'All he cares about are his damned profits. When Pershing refused to stand up to him, I knew then that I couldn't just sit back and do nothing. So I came after you.'

'How did you manage to trail us?' Cheyenne was baffled. He had made certain to leave no sign for a posse to follow. 'Only an Indian could have done that.'

'One of my early jobs with the bank was at Fort Belmont in the north,' Dunstan explained. 'My best customer was the Shoshone chief, Little Bear. His tribe had discovered gold on their land. Little Bear was shrewd enough to realize its value in a white man's world. So he made certain to bank what he recovered before the flood of prospectors invaded his lands. I sympathized with his predicament and made sure he was given a good interest rate on the deposits. In exchange he taught me how to hunt deer, track and read sign.'

'That's all very well,' cautioned Cheyenne, 'but going up against the Blackjacks is no Sunday afternoon turkey hunt. These guys shoot back and they aim to kill.'

Dunstan brushed aside his qualms with a shake of the hand. He tapped the Winchester resting in its boot. 'It is a prerequisite for all civilians working on a military base to be proficient in the use of firearams.'

Cheyenne was still not convinced. 'When it comes to the crunch, with all due respect Mr Dunstan, potting quail ain't the same as manhunting.' He paused to deliver his ultimatum. 'Are you prepared to shoot down a fellow human being without any hesitation?'

The bank manager levelled an incisive eye on to the younger man. 'These varmints are holding my daughter, sir. I will do anything it takes to get her safely out of their clutches.'

Cheyenne replied with a forthright nod of approval. 'Two men going up against that bunch was always going to be tough. Having you along sure increases our chances.' But he was adamant that the banking boss was now under his command. 'You do exactly as I say. When the chips are down, Sourdough and me give the orders. Agreed?'

'Without a doubt.' Then they shook hands on it.

Mounting up again, the three men swung off the narrow deer path into the forest of ponderosa pine that cloaked the slopes. They climbed steadily across the flank of the canyon pursuing a tortuous course ever higher through the green canopy. No light could penetrate through the dense trees. With little ground vegetation to hinder their mounts, progress was easier than expected.

Eventually, they emerged from the twilight world into bright sunshine. A wild rocky terrain stretched away to the horizon in all directions. It was an awesome tableau, beautiful and dramatic, yet not for the faint-hearted.

Dunstan was suddenly made fully cognizant of the dangerous situation in which he had placed himself. A momentary qualm assailed his churning stomach. Nervous eyes scanned the bleak wilderness. His concern was expressed in a tremulous voice. 'My fate is in your hands, sir. I trust that you are fully knowledgeable as to the route we should follow.'

Cheyenne threw a tight-lipped grimace at his partner. 'Are you sure you are up to this, Mr Dunstan?' he enquired. 'Best say now while there's still time for you to turn back. Once we reach Sawtooth Crack—'

Dunstan butted in with a firm rejoinder. 'I have no intention of backing out now. And you can count on me to use this' – he tapped the stock of the Winchester – 'when the time comes.'

'I ain't questioning your nerve,' Cheyenne assured the banker, 'I just need to know you're fully committed.'

'All the way.'

No more was said as Cheyenne led the way across the level top of the plateau.

It was an hour later that they approached the abrupt descent of Sawtooth Crack.

Cheyenne signalled a halt behind some boulders.

'Wait here while I suss out if'n a guard has been placed

up here,' he said, making his way up to a prominent ledge overlooking the entrance to the awesome fissure. Ten minutes passed before he returned.

'Looks like we're in luck,' he said mounting up. 'There is nobody guarding the Crack. Culpepper has done us a big favour that he's going to regret.'

They moved forward towards the eye-popping split. A stark rent in the otherwise solid wall at the back end of Gabbs Hole, the Crack had been caused by a cataclysmic fracturing of the rock in the distant past. The weakness had been exploited by constantly changing weather patterns. And now a steeply canting chute of loose stones led down into the Hole from above.

But it was no simple undertaking. Hazardous in the extreme, the descent was too steep to ride down. A zigzagging narrow trail had been stamped out by the Blackjacks during their time hiding out in the remote outpost below. As it was, extreme care was needed to avoid causing an avalanche in which they would be swept away to their deaths.

Peering down into the depths of the Crack, Dunstan felt his stomach lurch.

'Are you sure we can go down into that?' he blurted out.

Vertical walls of rock rose sheer on either side of the tight crevice. From where they now sat their horses on the brink of the abyss, it looked to be an impossible undertaking.

'We'll have to go on foot down that track,' Cheyenne replied, pointing out the faint impression in the stony surface that was little more than a footpath. 'But once we're below the lip, the grade eases. Then we can mount up again.' He grinned at the older man. 'Just close your eyes and keep hold of the chestnut's tail,' he advised. 'Your cayuse will do all the work by picking out the safest route. They are a sight better at it than us.'

'If you say so,' the banker muttered, although he was less than convinced.

Cheyenne led the way followed by Sourdough.

'Easy as falling off'n a log,' the old-timer chuckled.

Josiah Dunstan's heart was in his mouth as he took up the rear.

A fearful eye glanced up at the towering walls of sandstone looming on either side. The bright sunlight was blotted out plunging the chasm into deep shadow making the descent all the more menacing. The horses maintained a slow yet steady pace. Slowly, yet inexorably, they lost height. Dunstan was surprised that his horse was so sure-footed.

Eventually after what seemed to him like half a lifetime, they reached safer ground and were able to once again mount up.

'See?' Cheyenne chided his unexpected associate. 'Nothing to it.'

A half-hour later they were drawing near to the Blackjack encampment. A plume of smoke from the cabin dribbled above the line of willows that lined the small creek occupying the floor of the box canyon. The three men left their horses tethered and crept cautiously up to the edge of the clearing.

'My figuring is that by now, Culpepper will have sent a man to deliver his ultimatum to the town. He'll expect

146

everybody to be eaten up with grief.' Cheyenne had lowered his voice to a whisper. 'It won't have entered his devious mind that the upstanding people of Winnemucca would even consider putting the daughter of their leading citizen at risk. Respectable folks don't act that way.' A note of anger had crept into his acerbic tongue. 'We know now that some of these so-called decent folks are beneath contempt.'

'So how many are we up against, pard?' asked Sourdough thumbing shells into the loading bay of his Henry carbine.

'I think he'll have sent Mesa Quinn to town, him being the most educated of the gang. So that leaves Culpepper and two others in the cabin plus the one guarding the entrance. I'm assuming that he hasn't yet had time to recruit any new jaspers to make up for his losses.'

'And the messenger will be clapped in jail as soon as he arrives in town,' added Dunstan.

At that moment, the door of the cabin opened and somebody came out. They were all stunned to see that it was Jody. She headed across to a separate wooden building. Dunstan lumbered to his feet. He was about to call out when Cheyenne pulled him back down wrapping a hand across his mouth.

'Don't be such a durned fool,' he blazed angrily. 'Reveal our presence now and we're all done for. Culpepper or one of the others will be watching her every move. That's the larder where all the food is stored.'

So near yet so far.

As if to confirm his fears, Elko Boon came to the door and shouted across to the girl. 'Bring back a tin of peaches

147

as well as the coffee while you're there, gal.'

The outlaw's blunt order carried easily in the still air. He leaned on the edge of the cabin smoking a cigar until the girl returned. Cheyenne gritted his teeth. Like Dunstan, he was itching to let her know that help was at hand. But his hands were tied. Her ashen features were pinched and drawn, fear written indelibly across the gaunt face.

'So what's the plan?' asked Sourdough.

'They clearly don't expect Jody to make an escape bid,' he replied, shrugging his shoulders. 'Where could she go? Somehow we have to get her away from the cabin long enough to get away unscathed. I'm open to any ideas you guys can suggest,' he asked the others.

'Sooner or later, they're going to send her out to get water from the creek,' Sourdough offered. 'That's when we can grab her and skedaddle.'

'Sounds good to me,' enthused Cheyenne. 'What about you, Mr Dunstan?'

'I'll back you up with my rifle when those skunks come out of the cabin to see what's delaying her return,' said the banker. A glint of steel was reflected in his cold stare.

'The place for you is with your daughter, fella,' countered Sourdough. 'She's gonna need care and consideration after all she's been through. I should be the one to keep you covered.'

Cheyenne nodded. That seemed to be the best plan. All they had to do now was wait for the girl to emerge. But how long would that be? Every minute wasted added to their anxiety.

An hour passed after which Jackknife Stringer came out

of the cabin and mounted up.

'Looks like they are changing guards,' observed Sourdough. 'That leaves two in the cabin.'

Cheyenne consulted his watch. It read 4.53 p.m. – time for the evening meal to be prepared. And another two hours before sundown. Jody must emerge soon if'n they were to finish this business before dark.

Knuckles blanched, he gripped the stock of his rifle. His nerves were on edge willing that door to open and his beloved to come out holding a water pail. Worry drew the sun-crinkled skin tight across his face.

They had another ten minutes to wait before his prayers were answered.

The girl wandered disconsolately down to the creek, unaware that rescue was at hand. Sourdough took up his position facing the door of the cabin while his two associates crept along the side of the creek behind the line of dwarf willows.

Still within sight of the cabin, the girl stooped down and began filling the pail. From their place of concealment, Dunstan made a hissing sound between his teeth to attract her attention The girl appeared not to have heard. Perhaps her mind had shut down. He repeated the earnest call louder. This time she raised her head.

'Over here, Jody,' came the urgent entreaty. 'It's me, your pa.' She looked across, eyes bulging wide, unable to comprehend what she was seeing. 'Cheyenne is here with me as well. We've come to get you out of this mess.'

Cheyenne took over. 'Just move across into the cover of these willows, Jody,' he said slowly and in a measured tone. 'But keep it slow and easy. We don't want those critters getting wind that something's afoot.'

Every nerve in her body screamed at Jody to run across to join her loved ones. But she forced herself to remain calm. With a feigned air of nonchalance, she stood up and sidled across to the trees. Once inside, she fell into the arms of her father. Tears that had been locked away suddenly burst out.

'It's going to be fine,' burbled her equally relieved father. 'We'll get you out of here.'

But Cheyenne knew that this was no time for histrionics. They had to get away before the balloon went up. None too delicately, he bundled the girl through the tree cover to where the horses were tethered. He pushed Jody on to his horse and climbed up behind.

They would have to ride double.

That was when shots rang out. They were coming from across the far side of the creek.

It was Windy Macaw and he had spotted them. The outlaw had arrived back earlier than expected from his guard duty at the entrance to the Hole. Clearly shocked to see intruders skulking by the creek, the gunman let loose with his shooter while still mounted.

FOURTEEN

BIG-NOSE PLAYS DIRTY

A crack shot might have taken out his target. But Macaw was no Wild Bill Hickok.

One bullet plucked at Cheyenne's sleeve. But it was a lucky shot. The others went wide. As the outlaw galloped across the shallow watercourse, Dunstan took careful aim with his rifle and fired. Only the one shot was needed to lift the charging rider out of the saddle. It was the first man he had killed. But this was no time for vacillation. The noisy arrival of Windy Macaw had alerted the remaining Blackjacks in the cabin.

'You guys get going,' shouted Sourdough, as he pumped a couple of shots across the open sward. 'I'll keep you covered.'

'Don't stick around for too long, old buddy,' replied his anxious partner. 'Just stay long enough to delay them.

Then you come a-running, savvy?'

A lift of an arm was the sole acknowledgement as the old timer continued firing at the cabin.

Rafe Culpepper was given a brief glimpse of his hostage disappearing amongst the trees by the creek. He quickly reached the conclusion that his nemesis had returned for the purpose of rescuing the girl. A rabid curse erupted from his distorted mouth as he cursed his stupidity.

It was equally clear that Brady had not used the main entrance to Gabbs Hole. Then the truth struck him in the kisser with the force of a swinging haymaker.

Sawtooth Crack! He had forgotten all about the back door.

But he was not beaten yet.

Casting a wary eye down the slope, he could see the body of Windy Macaw. The creek was turning red from the dead outlaw's blood. But at least there only appeared to be a handful of rescuers. And one of them had been left behind as a delaying tactic while the girl was spirited away. Well, they weren't going to outsmart Rafe Culpepper.

He turned to Boon who was looking stunned at the sudden change in their circumstances.

'There's some jasper down by the creek,' he snapped out. 'He's been left to keep us pinned down while the other varmints escape with the girl by way of Sawtooth Crack. You climb out the back window and circle round behind him. I'll keep him occupied from up here.'

Boon looked at him, a dull expression clouding the outlaw's skeletal visage.

'Snap out of it, yuh dumb cluck,' he yelled. 'Do as I say if'n you want to see another dawn.' The heavyweight

Remington Rider pointing his way was enough to encourage Elko Boon to comply.

'Sure, boss,' he muttered, hustling towards the back room. 'It was seeing poor old Windy's life blood flowing down the creek that shook me.'

'He's dead,' rapped Culpepper. 'But we're still here as long as you carry out my orders. And let's hope that Stringer gets the message as well.' He was assuming that the man guarding the entrance to Gabbs Hole would have heard the gunfire and hot-footed back down the canyon.

Elko Boon snuck out the back window of the cabin and scuttled behind some rocks. No gunfire came his way which meant that the guy down by the creek was unaware of the subterfuge. Boon smiled. This was more like it. He continued behind the cluster of rocks before moving cautiously down into the scattering of willows beside the creek.

Intermittent spates of gunfire continued to hold the guy's attention enabling Boon to edge up behind his quarry.

The rattle of gunfire spurred the escaping trio onward. In spite of one horse having a double load, they made good time back to the bottom of Sawtooth Crack. The menacing fissure loomed ominously above their heads.

Suddenly, as if a door had been slammed shut on a noisy gathering, the shooting at the cabin terminated. A tense silence ensued. Who had survived? Cheyenne prayed hard that his old buddy would soon come galloping along the bottom of Gabbs Hole. But they had to keep moving. All too soon, they were forced to dismount and continue on foot.

Every few minutes, Cheyenne scanned his backtrail, but there was no sign of his partner.

Elko Boon was so elated at having a sitting target to aim at that he forgot to heed where his feet were treading. A dry twig snapped. The other man instantly swung round. He levered off two shots before Boon knew what had hit him. A startled look pinched the outlaw's twisted maw as he staggered back clutching at the twin holes in his chest.

Sourdough also made the mistake of standing up to check the backshooter was finished. It was to be a fatal miscalculation. Always one to take advantage of other people's errors, Culpepper drilled the unfortunate old prospector in the back. Big-Nose didn't bother to check the bodies. He dashed over to his horse and leapt into the saddle.

Culpepper should have realized that the game was up. The Blackjacks were a spent force. He could have ridden away taking Stringer with him and established a new gang some place else. But all the ageing brigand could see was that Judas of a double-crosser who had outwitted him. Rafe Culpepper was eaten up with hatred and the lust to even the score. And by getting the girl back, he would still hold a winning hand.

He spurred his horse along the floor of the canyon in pursuit of the fleeing fugitives. On the far side, riding almost parallel, was Jackknife Stringer. Culpepper signalled to the blade-wielder to join him. Stringer splashed across.

'What's happened, boss?' the outlaw gasped out. 'I heard the shooting and figured those dudes from Winnemucca had somehow located the Crack.'

'It's Brady and he's managed to get hold of the girl,' rasped Culpepper, the wind bending back the brim of his hat. Ragged black hair streaming behind, he looked just like his buccaneering hero, Blackbeard the Pirate. 'But we can catch them at the Crack.'

Urging their mounts to the gallop, the two outlaws streaked along the edge of the shallows. They reached the base of Sawtooth Crack while Cheyenne and his associates were only halfway up the acclivitous grade. Riding double had slowed them down considerably.

While chasing after the fugitives, Culpepper had been working out how best to end this débâcle in his favour. He could see them clearly now out in the open meandering like ants up the tortuous zig-zagging path. A couple of shots loosed from his rifle instantly brought them to a halt. He could hear the bullets zipping and whining off the rocks.

The three escapees were forced to duck down amongst the plethora of boulders choking the Crack.

'While I keep these dudes pinned down from below,' Culpepper informed his sidekick, 'I want you to sneak up the far side of the Crack. When I call Brady out and challenge him to a duel, that's when you take him out. But wait until I raise my arm before opening fire. With him down, the other critter will be easy meat. I'll give you time to get in position before I make my play.'

'Sure thing, boss,' Stringer concurred. 'It sounds like a good plan.'

'Don't let them spot you.'

Stringer nodded then slunk off behind some trees.

For the next ten minutes, Culpepper kept up a steady

rate of fire that effectively prevented the runaways from moving.

It was a stalemate. Just what Culpepper wanted.

'Can you hear me, Brady?' he shouted. The strident bark echoed back from the confines of the narrow ravine.

'I hear you, Rafe,' came back the somewhat depressed response. 'What's on your mind?'

'You ain't going nowhere, mister. Try to move and I can pick you off easier than a Thanksgiving turkey shoot.' He paused waiting for a reaction. He grinned when none came. 'So I have a proposition.'

This time, as expected there was a reply.

'What are you suggesting?'

'You're stuck up there with no place to go. I'm down here. If'n I go back to the cabin for some supplies, you can escape and bring the law down here. I can't let you do that. I propose we meet halfway and have it out. Man to man. A fair duel between two old buddies. The gang is finished. There's only me left.'

'What happened to Stringer?' came back the sceptical retort.

'He's run out on me, just like that no-account Kid Syrillo.'

'I brought him in . . . over the back of his horse. He's resting up with the Winnemucca undertaker.'

'Well ain't that something.' There was genuine respect in Culpepper's voice. 'I never should have taken that rat on. Too late now though. It's just us two. So how about it, Cheyenne? Are you game to take me on?'

'I'll talk it over with my associates.'

'Don't be too long. It'll be dark soon. And you know

how cold it can get at nights in the Monte Cristos.' A macabre chuckle rippled around the bleak rock terrain.

'You can't go out there,' protested Jody. 'I don't want to lose you now. Surely we could walk out of here once the sun goes down.'

Cheyenne shook his head. 'Not being able to see our way forward in this wild terrain is asking for trouble. We could easily break a leg or walk off a cliff edge to our deaths. And Culpepper knows that. I have to go along with his suggestion. Maybe I'm faster than him. I don't know. It's never been an issue before.' He sucked in lungfuls of mountain air. 'We'll soon find out.'

He turned to address the outlaw. 'I agree to your proposal, Rafe. But let Jody and her father climb out of here. This is just between the two of us.'

'All right, but no funny business,' was the blunt reply. 'I'm coming up to meet you. We both keep our hands well clear of the hardware until the rules of engagement are settled.'

'Still playing by the rules, Rafe?'

'It's the only way, buddy.'

The two men emerged from cover and began to slowly and carefully pick their way amongst the loose scree. Culpepper narrowed his eyes searching for the presence of Jackknife Stringer. Suddenly his body tensed as a patch of green swam into view amidst the sea of oranges and reds. A grim smile flickered across his face. A momentary acknowledgement that all was ready.

Nothing else moved. Neither a bird nor a critter disturbed the tranquil calm of Gabbs Hole. A sanguinary illusion that was about to be shattered.

'That's far enough.'

Culpepper's brusque call brought Cheyenne to a stumbling halt.

'What happened to my partner, Rafe?' he rasped, trying to stifle the nervous tremor that threatened to overawe him.

'The old guy didn't make it. Pity I had to backshoot him.'

Cheyenne gulped. He had expected it. But the grim revelation still came as a shock to his twanging nerves. 'So how we gonna play this?' he forced himself to enquire.

'Only one way it can be played.'

Culpepper then casually lifted his arm.

A single rifle shot followed. It bounced off the rock walls sounding like a manic Gatling gun. But Brady was still standing. Culpepper looked across to where his confederate was concealed. A green shirt lay draped across a rock. His mouth hung open. What in thunder had gone wrong? Frantic eyes probed the rocky enclave.

Then he saw a man stand up clutching a smoking rifle to his chest.

'Your heinous plan to bushwhack my future son-in-law has failed, Mr Culpepper,' the man called down in a firm voice. It was possessed of cultured overtones that could only belong to the girl's father, the bank manager. 'I have learnt a lot in the last few days,' continued Dunstan making sure that he was not exposed. 'And the most important lesson is not to trust a blackguard such as youself. It appears that my caution has been rewarded.'

'And now it's our turn, Rafe,' Cheyenne added barely above a whisper. 'And this time we truly will discover who

158

is the faster gunhand.'

Jody watched from higher up Sawtooth Crack. Her heart was in her mouth as the two antagonists faced each other. She wanted to look away but forced herself to observe the gruesome duel.

Hours passed on the steep slopes of Sawtooth Crack, in effect little more than a minute. Then smoke issued from the two pistols. Cheyenne stumbled back falling to the ground. Jody's scream sounded like the baying of a thousand coyotes. Seconds later, his adversary keeled over on to his face and lay still.

The girl stumbled down the narrow path oblivious to the danger. Halfway down she was joined by her father. Drawing nearer to the scene of the recent conflict, she could see a patch of red mushrooming on her man's shoulder. It was only a flesh wound so not life-threatening.

Cheyenne struggled to his feet and walked over to where Culpepper was lying. He rolled the outlaw on to his back. He was still breathing, but only just clinging to the shreds of life.

'Seems like . . . you have the beating . . . of me . . . old buddy,' he croaked out. Blood issued from between clenched teeth.

'You played a false game, Rafe,' said Cheyenne. 'That's not your way.'

'Guess I got carried away. . . . I knew all along . . . you were . . . the better man. I've enjoyed . . riding with you, Cheyenne. A pity things . . . didn't work out. . . .' A spasm of pain wracked the heaving torso. 'So long—'

Then Big-Nose Rafe Culpepper cashed in his chips for the last time.

'So long, Rafe,' whispered Cheyenne.

There was no sorrow in the final parting. The guy had killed his partner and almost led to him being lynched. Nevertheless, the final showdown had given him no pleasure. Just a feeling that the fresh start for which he yearned could now come to fruition.

It was a somewhat chastened trio who finally crested the last rise at the top of Sawtooth Crack. There was no hallooing and cheering. Only a feeling of quiet relief that the past days and weeks were over.

Jody was the first to speak as they mounted up and rode away.

'Did you mean what you said before, Pa?' She gulped nervously before continuing. 'About Cheyenne becoming your son-in-law?' The girl's question was hesitant, the utterance stilted and doubtful of what she had heard.

But Dunstan had no such reservations. 'Nothing would give me greater pleasure than to see you walk down the aisle with this man.'

Coy smiles passed between Cheyenne Brady and his beloved. They gingerly held hands.

'I'll leave you two love birds alone to discuss the future,' the bank manger said breezily as he spurred on ahead.